A TREASURY
of CHILDREN'S
LITERATURE

A TREASURY
of CHILDREN'S
LITERATURE

A TREASURY
of CHILDREN'S
LITERATURE

Edited by Armand Eisen

Ariel Books

Houghton Mifflin Company
Boston 1992

Library of Congress Cataloging-in-Publication Data

A Treasury of children's literature/edited by Armand Eisen.
p.   cm.
"Ariel Books."
Summary: A collection of traditional and original stories and
poems by such authors as Aesop, and Lewis Carroll, including
excerpts from "The Wind in the Willows" and "Peter Pan."
ISBN 0-395-53349-X
1. Children's literature   [1. Literature–Collections.]
I. Eisen, Armand
PZ5. T7475 1992
[Fic]–dc20   92-2847
                                                          CIP
                                                          AC

Contents

Traditional Stories
Retold by Sheila Black

GOLDILOCKS AND THE THREE BEARS
Illustrated by Lynn Bywaters
12

SLEEPING BEAUTY
Illustrated by Ruth Sanderson
20

THREE BILLY GOATS GRUFF
Illustrated by Robyn Officer
36

JACK AND THE BEANSTALK
Illustrated by Elizabeth Miles
39

THE THREE LITTLE PIGS
Illustrated by Robyn Officer
51

LITTLE RED RIDING HOOD
Illustrated by Lynn Bywaters
58

Aesop's Fables
Retold by Sheila Black
Illustrated by Richard Bernal
70

Grimm's Fairy Tales
Retold by Sheila Black

CINDERELLA
Illustrated by Robyn Officer   78

HANSEL AND GRETEL
Illustrated by Scott Gustafson   86

RAPUNZEL
Illustrated by Erin Augenstine   95

THE FROG PRINCE
Illustrated by Robyn Officer   101

THE BREMENTOWN MUSICIANS
Illustrated by Scott Gustafson   107

SNOW WHITE
Illustrated by Lynn Bywaters   112

RUMPELSTILTSKIN
Illustrated by Gary Cooley   128

Mother Goose's Nursery Rhymes
Illustrated by Allen Atkinson   136

Children's Classics

THE MAD TEA-PARTY
From *Alice's Adventures in Wonderland* by Lewis Carroll
Illustrated by S. Michele Wiggens   146

THE CAT AND THE FOX AGAIN
From *Pinocchio* by Carlo Collodi, excerpted by Della Rowland
Illustrated by Scott Gustafson   156

THE PIPER AT THE GATES OF DAWN
From *The Wind in the Willows* by Kenneth Grahame
Illustrated by Troy Howell   162

TOYLAND and THE CAPITAL OF TOYLAND
From *The Nutcracker* by E.T.A. Hoffman
Illustrated by Carter Goodrich   174

"HOOK OR ME THIS TIME"
From *Peter Pan* by James M. Barrie
Illustrated by Scott Gustafson   188

ROBERT LOUIS STEVENSON'S
A Child's Garden of Verses
Illustrated by Arlene Klemushin   204

American Tales
Retold by Sheila Black

BR'ER RABBIT
Illustrated by Richard Bernal   214

JOHNNY APPLESEED
Illustrated by Gary Gianni   219

JOHN HENRY
Illustrated by Gary Gianni   225

PAUL BUNYAN
Illustrated by Richard Bernal   234

The Night Before Christmas
By Clement C. Moore
Illustrated by Scott Gustafson   246

Hans Christian Andersen's Fairy Tales
Retold by Sheila Black

THE UGLY DUCKLING
Illustrated by Elizabeth Miles   260

THE NIGHTINGALE
Illustrated by Erin Augenstine   270

THE STEADFAST TIN SOLDIER
Illustrated by Michael Montgomery   278

THE EMPEROR'S NEW CLOTHES
Illustrated by Richard Walz   284

THE PRINCESS AND THE PEA
Illustrated by Robyn Officer   290

THE LITTLE MATCH GIRL
Illustrated by Erin Augenstine   293

THUMBELINA
Illustrated by Robyn Officer   296

Traditional Tales

Goldilocks and the Three Bears

T here was once a family of bears who lived in a cozy cottage in the woods. There was a great big Papa Bear, a medium-sized Mama Bear, and a little tiny Baby Bear.
One morning Mama Bear cooked them some porridge for breakfast. As the porridge was too hot to eat, the Three Bears decided to take a walk in the woods while it cooled.

They had not been gone long when a little girl named Goldilocks came along. She had been picking flowers and had wandered into the woods. When she saw the Three Bears' cottage, she smiled and clapped her hands. "How pretty!" she cried. "I wonder who lives there?" She stood on her toes and peeked in the window. There didn't seeem to be anyone home so Goldilocks opened the door and went right inside!

12

The first thing she saw was the table set with three bowls of porridge: a great big bowl for Papa Bear, a medium-sized bowl for Mama Bear, and a tiny little bowl for Baby Bear. "Oh, that porridge smells good!" Goldilocks said. Then, as she was feeling a little hungry, she picked up a spoon and tasted the porridge in the great big bowl.

"Ouch!" she cried, dropping the spoon. "That porridge is much too hot!"

So she tasted the porridge in the medium-sized bowl. But that porridge was much too cold.

Then she tasted the porridge in the tiny little bowl. "Mmmmm," she said. "This porridge is just right!" So she ate it all up!

Then Goldilocks saw three chairs set before the fire: a great big chair for Papa Bear, a medium-sized chair for Mama Bear, and a tiny little chair for Baby Bear. "Oh, it would be nice to sit down for a while!" Goldilocks thought.

So she climbed into the great big chair that belonged to Papa Bear. "Oh, no!" she said. "That chair is much too hard."

Then she sat in Mama Bear's medium-sized chair. "Oh, no," she said. "That chair is much too soft!"

Next, she sat in Baby Bear's tiny little chair. "Ahh," she said with a smile. "This chair is just right!"

Just then there was a loud crack! and the little chair broke right through!

Goldilocks stood up and dusted herself off. Then she climbed upstairs to the bedroom. There she saw three beds all in a row.

"Oh," she said, yawning, "I am feeling sleepy."

So she pulled down the covers and climbed into Papa Bear's great big bed. But she quickly jumped down. "That bed is much too hard," she said.

Then she tried Mama Bear's medium-sized bed. But it was too soft.

So she climbed into Baby Bear's tiny little bed. It was just right. Soon Goldilocks was fast asleep!

A little while later the Three Bears returned from their walk. They were feeling very hungry and were looking forward to eating the nice bowls of tasty porridge.

Suddenly Papa Bear cried out in his great big voice, "Someone has been eating *my* porridge."

Then Mama Bear cried out in her medium-sized voice, "Someone has been eating *my* porridge!"

And Baby Bear cried out in his tiny little voice, "Someone has been eating *my* porridge. And they've eaten it all up."

Then the Three Bears saw their three chairs near the fireplace.

"Someone has been sitting in *my* chair!" Papa Bear said in his great big voice.

"And someone has been sitting in *my* chair," Mama Bear said in her medium-sized voice.

"Someone has been sitting in *my* chair," Baby Bear cried in his tiny little voice. "And now it's broken!"

Then the Three Bears went upstairs to the bedroom.

"Someone has been sleeping in *my* bed!" Papa Bear shouted in his great big voice.

"And someone has been sleeping in *my* bed!" Mama Bear exclaimed in her medium-sized voice.

"Someone has been sleeping in *my* bed," Baby Bear squeaked in his tiny little voice. "AND HERE SHE IS!"

Just then Goldilocks woke up. When she saw the Three Bears stand-ing around her, she leaped off the bed and ran down the stairs and out the door. She didn't stop until she was all the way back home.

And the Three Bears never saw Goldilocks again!

Sleeping Beauty

⸺ ❧ ⸺

Once upon a time there lived a king and queen who longed for a child more than anything. Yet no child came. Then one day as the queen was bathing, a frog hopped out of the water and said to her, "Oh, queen, before the year has ended, you will give birth to a daughter."

Just as the frog had predicted, before the year was out, the queen gave birth to a beautiful baby girl.

The king was overjoyed and ordered a great feast. He invited not only his relatives and all the great nobles of the kingdom but also the fairies who lived in the land. He hoped that once they saw the beautiful girl they, too, would love her and be sure to treat her well. There were thirteen fairies in the kingdom, but as the king knew of only twelve, he sent no invitation to the last one.

The feast was very splendid, and when it was over, the twelve fairies came forward to present the child with magical gifts. The first gave the princess beauty, the second, goodness. The third promised her riches, and

the fourth, charm. The fifth gave her the gift of quick wit, and on it
went, until the little princess had every gift one could wish for.

No sooner had the eleventh fairy given her gift, than the
thirteenth fairy suddenly appeared. She was furious
that she had not been invited, and she cried
out in a terrible voice, "When the princess
is fifteen, she will prick herself on a

spindle and fall dead!" Then without another word, she turned and swept out of the hall.

The king and the queen were heartbroken. But then the twelfth fairy, who still had not given her gift, stepped forward. "I cannot take back the curse," she said quietly, "but I can soften it. The princess will not die. Instead she will fall into a deep sleep that will last for one hundred years."

The king, wishing to spare his daughter even this misfortune, gave orders that all the spindles in the kingdom be burned, and that no one be allowed to keep even a single one.

The princess grew, and all the gifts of the fairies were fulfilled. She became so beautiful, intelligent, and pure of heart that everyone who saw her could not help but love her.

It so happened that on the day of her fifteenth birthday, her parents paid a visit to a neighboring prince. The princess was left alone in the castle. She amused herself by wandering through the numerous rooms and halls. She peered into cramped attics and explored tall, forgotten towers. She discovered a dusty spiral staircase and climbed the narrow steps round and round until she came to a little door. A rusty key was in the lock, and when the princess turned it, the door sprang open.

Inside the small room an old woman sat with a spindle and distaff, busily spinning flax into thread.

"How do you do?" said the princess. "Pray, tell me, Grandmother, what are you doing?" for she had never seen a spindle or a distaff before.

"I am spinning, dear child," the old woman replied.

The spindle was twirling and bobbing so merrily. "May I try?" asked the girl.

The old woman nodded, and the princess reached out her hand. But no sooner had she touched the spindle than it pricked her finger.

The moment she was pricked, she fell upon the bed and sank into a deep sleep. This sleep spread throughout the castle. The king and queen, who were just returning home, fell asleep in the doorway. All the pages and courtiers and guards and watchmen fell asleep where they stood. The dogs fell asleep in the courtyard, and the horses fell asleep in their stables.

So did the pigeons on the roof, and even the flies on the wall—all sound asleep.

In the kitchen, the cook, who was about to pull the scullery boy's ears for stealing a biscuit, dropped off to sleep. But the scullery boy didn't run away, for he slumbered, too. The kitchen maid, who was sitting at the hearth, basting chickens on the spit, closed her eyes and lay her head across her knees. The chickens on the spit stopped turning and sizzling, and even the fire stopped flickering and fell asleep. The wind fell silent, and not a leaf, not even a pinch of dust, stirred in the king's castle.

Soon a great brier hedge began to grow around the castle. It grew thick and high until nothing could be seen of the castle, not even the flags that waved from its towers. Over the years various stories spread about the enchanted brier hedge and the castle behind it. Some people even said that a beautiful princess lay sleeping there.

Princes from kingdoms near and far came and tried to cut through the brier hedge to find the sleeping princess. But when the young men tried to pass through, the hedge's thorny branches clasped tightly around them. The princes became trapped in the brier hedge and died miserably.

One day, when the hundred years were almost up, a young and handsome prince happened to visit the kingdom. He had heard an old man telling the story of the brier hedge and the hidden castle and the beautiful princess who had been sleeping there for countless years.

"How I should like to see her!" the prince said. "Where is this place and how do I get there?" The old man then told him that many princes had tried to find the princess, and that they had all been caught in the brier hedge and died. But no matter how much the old man warned the prince against going to the castle, he refused to listen. "I am not afraid," the prince said. "I want to see the beautiful Sleeping Beauty," for that is how the princess was now known.

So the prince mounted his horse and rode to the castle.

The hundred years had passed, and the day had come when the princess was to awaken. As the prince drew near the brier hedge, the thorns melted away. In their place appeared large and beautiful flowers, and the branches parted to allow the prince to pass. With each step he took, a path opened before him. And so the prince walked through the hedge and into the castle.

In the courtyard, he saw horses and dogs lying fast asleep and guards and watchmen slumbering against the walls with their swords beside them. On the roof pigeons slept with their heads tucked under their wings. The flies on the wall were still all fast asleep. In the kitchen, the cook still held out his hand to grab the scullery boy by the ears. And the kitchen maid sat with her head in her lap in front of the hearth.

The prince walked deeper into the castle. In the hall he found the pages and courtiers sleeping where they stood, and the king and queen asleep in the doorway. He went farther, until the silence of the palace grew so great that he could hear the pounding of his own heart and the blood rushing through his veins.

At last, he came to the tower and climbed the long, dusty spiral stair-case to the room where Sleeping Beauty lay.

Then he saw her. She looked so beautiful that the prince could not take his eyes from her. He bent down and kissed her. At his touch, Sleeping Beauty opened her eyes and looked at him with great tenderness.

Then he took her hand, and together they descended the stairs and went into the castle.

As they entered the front hall, the king and queen and all the pages and courtiers woke up and looked at each other in amazement. The horses in the courtyard stood up and stamped their hooves. The dogs began to bark and wag their tails. The pigeons pulled their heads from under their wings and, twittering and cooing, flew off into the fields. The flies began to crawl along the walls. In the kitchen the fire in the hearth sputtered and flared back to life. The cook reached out and tugged on the scullery boy's ears so hard that he cried out. And the kitchen maid began turning the chickens as they sizzled on the spit.

The wedding of Sleeping Beauty and her prince was celebrated with great joy and splendor. And they lived happily ever after.

Three Billy Goats Gruff

———— ❦ ————

O nce upon a time there were three billy goats who wished very much to climb up the hillside to where the grass was green and thick so that they might become fat. The name of all three was Gruff, and so they were called the Three Billy Goats Gruff.

To get up the hillside they had to cross a bridge over a rushing mountain stream. Under this bridge there lived a big ugly Troll.

The youngest Billy Goat Gruff came to the bridge first. Tap-tap, tap-tap went his little hooves as he ran across it. But when he was in the center of the bridge, the Troll called out in a great big voice, "Who's that crossing *my* bridge?"

"It's only me," said the first Billy Goat Gruff, in his not-very-loud little voice.

"Well, then, I'll eat you up!" the Troll replied.

"Oh, no! Please don't do that. I'm much too small and thin for you. Wait until my brother the second Billy Goat Gruff comes along. He's much bigger than I am."

As he was feeling rather hungry, the Troll agreed to wait.

Soon the second Billy Goat Gruff came to the bridge. Trip-trap, trip-trap went his middle-sized hooves as he ran across. But when he got to the center, the Troll called up in a great big voice, "Who's that crossing my bridge?"

"It's only me," the second Billy Goat Gruff said in his medium-sized voice.

"Well, then, I'll eat you up!" the Troll replied.

"Oh, no! Don't do that. Wait until the third Billy Goat Gruff comes along. He's much bigger than I am and just the right size for a fine Troll like you!"

The Troll was feeling very hungry by now, and so once again he agreed.

Soon the third Billy Goat Gruff came walking over the bridge. TRAMP, TRAMP, TRAMP went his great big hooves. "Who's that crossing my bridge?" the Troll called up in his great big voice.

And the third Billy Goat Gruff replied in an even bigger voice, "It's only ME!"

"Well, then," said the Troll, "I'll eat you up!"

"Come on, then," said the third Billy Goat Gruff, and he added:

"I've got two sharp horns
to poke your nose,
And lots of sharp teeth
to bite you all over,
And two big pronged hooves,
to break your bones!"

The Troll, who didn't really believe him, climbed up onto the bridge. The third Billy Goat Gruff butted the Troll with his horns and bit him with his teeth and kicked him with his hooves until the big ugly Troll fell into the mountain stream and was never heard of again!

As for the three Billy Goats Gruff, they went up the hillside and grew very fat indeed, and for all I know, they are still there!

Jack and the Beanstalk

⎯⎯⎯ ✦ ⎯⎯⎯

There was once a poor widow who lived in a little cottage with her son, Jack. Now, Jack was good-hearted and always meant well. Unfortunately, he was also careless and lazy. He did no work to help his poor mother, and so, little by little, they became very poor indeed.

At last, one day, the widow found that she and Jack would surely starve unless she sold the one possession she had left—an old cow named Milky White. One morning she went to her son. "Jack," she said, "take the cow to market and sell her for me as I'm too weak to go myself. But be sure and get a good price for her."

"Yes, Mother," Jack replied, and he set off, whistling as he went. He had not gone far when he met a butcher who was also on his way to the market. The butcher was carrying some strange, brightly colored beans in his hand. Jack could not help admiring them. So the butcher whispered to Jack that the beans were magic and soon persuaded the silly lad to trade his cow for them.

Jack was very proud of himself and ran home to show the beans to his mother. But when the widow learned what her son had done, she burst into tears. "Oh, Jack!" she cried. "How could you be such a fool? Now we will surely starve." And taking the beans, she threw them out the window.

Jack was truly sorry, but there was nothing to be done. That evening he and his mother had only dry bread for supper. Then they both went sadly to bed.

That night Jack could not sleep. "Tomorrow my poor mother will have nothing to eat," he thought miserably. "And it is all my fault."

When the sun rose, Jack got up and walked out into the garden. To his amazement, he saw that during the night the beans had grown into a giant beanstalk that climbed all the way up into the clouds! It was so thick and leafy it made a kind of ladder, and Jack stared at it in awe.

He ran to fetch his mother, and they both gazed in wonder at the giant beanstalk. "I wonder where it goes," Jack said at last. "I think I will climb it and find out!"

His mother begged him not to, but Jack refused to listen. "I am sure there is something wonderful up there," he said, and so he began to climb.

Up he went, higher and higher, until everything below him—his mother's cottage and the village and even the church steeple—looked small enough to fit into his hand, and still he could not see to the top of the beanstalk. He climbed so high he dared not look down for fear it would make him dizzy. At last he poked his head up through the white clouds and found himself at the top of the beanstalk.

He stepped off the beanstalk into a strange and beautiful land. There were woods all around and green pastures where cows and sheep grazed. A stream of crystal-clear water ran before him, and across it, Jack saw a great castle of stone.

As he was staring at it, someone tapped him on the shoulder. It was a lady dressed in a long red gown trimmed all over with fur. She wore a hat to match, and her long hair streamed down over her shoulders.

"Good day, ma'am," said Jack. "Is that your castle?"

"No," the lady replied. "But listen closely and I will tell you who it belongs to."

"Yes?" said Jack.

"A noble knight once lived in that castle with his wife and baby son. He was a good man and loved by all, and he also had many rare and wonderful treasures. A giant, who lived nearby, heard of the knight's good fortune and became very jealous of him. One day, he went to the castle, snuck in, and killed the good knight while he lay sleeping. Luckily, the wife and the baby were out, so the giant did not kill them, too. However, he seized the castle and all that was in it. The baby's nurse, who had managed to escape, warned the lady of what had happened. And so the lady fled with her child to the nurse's house. The old nurse died soon afterward, and the poor lady has lived there in poverty ever since. Jack, the lady is your mother, and the good knight was your father. The castle was his and should by rights be yours."

Jack could hardly believe his ears. "Mine?" he said. "Oh, my poor mother. But tell me, what should I do?"

"You must win it back for your mother. But I must warn you it will be a difficult and dangerous task."

"I do not mind that," said Jack. "Only tell me how I must go about it."

"You must get into the castle somehow and steal from the giant a hen that lays golden eggs, two bags of gold, and a harp that talks. Then all will be well."

At that, the lady in red vanished, and Jack knew then that she must be a fairy.

He decided to do as she said without any delay. Boldly he strode to the giant's castle and rang the bell. The door was quickly answered by a great big giantess with three eyes—one was right in the middle of her forehead.

"Ah," she cried as soon as she saw Jack, and then she dragged him inside by the ears.

"Wait," Jack squeaked in terror. But the giantess didn't seem to hear him.

"I am so tired of my life here," she sighed. "Work, work from morning till night. At last, I shall have someone to help me. You can sharpen my knives and polish my boots and even help me make the fire, for that is a task I cannot abide. Of course, I will have to hide you when the giant is home, for there is nothing he likes better than a nice roasted Englishman for supper."

When Jack heard that he felt a little less frightened. "I will gladly help you," he said. "Only be sure to keep me well hidden from your husband, for I shouldn't like to be eaten at all!"

"Never fear," said the giantess. "I shall hide you in my wardrobe. The giant never looks in there. Now go on in and be quick about it. I hear him coming now." Then she opened the huge wardrobe in the hall and shoved Jack inside. At that moment the giant came stomping up the stairs, and each footstep was as loud as a cannon firing. Jack peered through the keyhole as a voice like thunder cried:

"Fe, fi, fo, fum!
I smell the blood of an Englishman.
Be he alive or be he dead,
I'll crush his bones to make my bread!"

"I smell a man!" the giant hollered at his wife. "Catch him and roast him for my breakfast."

"You must be getting foolish in your old age," cried his wife, almost as loudly. "That's not a man you smell, it's just a nice flock of sheep I've roasted for your breakfast."

Then she set a plate in front of him with twenty whole roasted sheep on it. The giant smiled and began to eat and forgot all about wanting the blood of an Englishman for breakfast. When he had eaten his fill, he went out for a walk. The giantess let Jack out of the wardrobe, and he helped with her chores all day long.

When evening came, the giantess hid him away again. Soon the giant came thundering up the stairs for his supper. Jack watched through

the keyhole as the giant ate six cows and twenty-seven chickens, forking the chickens whole into his great big mouth. When he was finished eating, the giant called to his wife, "Bring me the hen that lays the golden eggs."

The giantess went away and soon returned carrying a little red hen. She set it down in front of the giant and went off to bed.

The giant picked up the little hen and said, "Lay!" Instantly the little hen laid an egg of pure gold. "Lay!" the giant said again. And again the hen laid a gold egg. Then he said it a third time and she did so again.

"That must be the hen the fairy spoke of," Jack thought. "And it must have belonged to my father once."

Then, as Jack watched through the keyhole, the giant set the hen down, closed his big black eyes, and fell fast asleep, snoring so loudly the great stone walls shook.

When he was sure the giant wouldn't wake up, Jack crept from the wardrobe. Grabbing the little red hen, he tiptoed out to the kitchen and slipped out the back door. Then he raced as fast as he could back to the beanstalk and climbed down, holding the hen under his arm.

His mother was overjoyed to see him come back alive. And she was even happier when he told her what had happened and gave her the little red hen. Now, she said, their worries were over, and they would once again be rich and happy.

For a time they lived pleasantly, but then Jack began to think about the beanstalk again. At last, he decided he must climb up it one more time. But first he dyed his hair and disguised himself so the giantess would not recognize him. When he rang the bell, she dragged him inside as before and again hid him in the wardrobe. "The last boy I let in was a thief," she said. "But you have an honest face. However, you must be very quiet or the giant will surely eat you."

Soon the giant came in and shouted as before:

"Fe, fi, fo, fum!
I smell the blood of an Englishman.
Be he alive or be he dead,
I'll crush his bones to make my bread."

"How ridiculous you are," said his wife. "That is only some nice big bullocks I've roasted for your supper." Then she set before him a dish piled high with steaming meat.

The giant was quite satisfied and ate the bullocks as easily as if they had been sparrows. "Now," he said when he had eaten his fill, "bring me my moneybags for I would like to count my gold before I sleep." Soon she came back with two huge sacks slung over her shoulders, then she went off to bed.

The giant opened the sacks and began to pour out heaps and heaps of glittering gold coins. Jack's eyes grew wider and wider as he peered at all the gold. "That, too, must have belonged to my father once," he thought. At last, tired of counting gold and more gold, the giant put the coins back in the big sacks. Then he leaned back in his chair and was soon fast asleep, snoring so loudly that it sounded as though the whole world was crashing down.

Jack tiptoed out of the wardrobe. He picked up the sacks of coins, which were almost too heavy for him to carry. Then he staggered to the beanstalk and climbed down as fast as he could. When he got back to his mother's cottage, he set the bags of gold on the table before her. "This is the gold the giant stole from my father," he said. His mother was happy to see it returned to them, but she begged Jack never to go to the giant's castle again. "We have all we could wish for now," she said. Jack agreed, but after some time, he made up his mind to climb up the beanstalk one more time.

So, disguising himself again, up he went and was soon ringing the bell of the castle once more. The giantess answered the door. "Ah," she said. "The last two boys who came here were thieves, but I must have someone to help me with all my chores and you look honest to me." Then she dragged him inside and hid him in the big wardrobe. Presently the giant came marching home, and as he came through the door, he roared:

"Fe, fi, fo, fum!
I smell the blood of an Englishman.
Be he alive or be he dead,
I'll crush his bones to make my bread."

"You are so stupid," shouted his wife. "You just smell the nice mutton stew I've cooked for your supper." Then she set down a bowl of stew as big as a tub in front of the hungry giant.

When the giant had eaten his fill, he called, "Wife, bring me my harp, for I'd like a little music."

His wife soon brought him a harp made of gold and sparkling with rubies and diamonds. When she went for a walk, the giant drew the harp toward him. "Play!" he said.

The harp began to play a lovely sad melody.

"Play something livelier," said the giant.

The harp began to play a merry jig.

"Play me a lullabye," the giant said then. And the harp began to play the most charming lullabye in the world. As the giant listened to it, his eyes grew heavy, and soon he was fast asleep, snoring so loudly it sounded like a great drum beating in the sky.

Jack slipped out of the wardrobe, silently crept to the gold harp, and picked it up. He was about to run out the door with it, when the harp suddenly shouted, "Master! Master!"

With a start, the giant woke up and with a scream of rage came running after Jack. Luckily, Jack was very nimble and jumped out the door and skipped over the stream. However, the giant was close on his heels, and Jack might have been caught had not the giant happened to trip over a stone. He fell flat on his face, giving Jack just enough time to reach the beanstalk.

Quick as lightning, Jack went climbing down. But just as he was about to reach his mother's cottage, he saw the giant begin climbing down after him. "Mother!" Jack cried. "Quick! Fetch me the axe." His mother came running with it. Jack grabbed it and with a single blow cut through the beanstalk. The beanstalk came crashing down, down, down, and then with a great thud that made the ground shake and the sky groan, the giant landed dead at their feet.

Just then the fairy appeared before them. "Jack," she said, "you have acted like a true knight's son, and now that you have won back your inheritance, you and your mother will live happily ever after. The castle has been returned to earth, and now it and everything in it are yours again."

So Jack and his mother let the fairy lead them to where the great stone castle now stood. And there, as the fairy promised, they lived happily for the rest of their days.

The Three Little Pigs

O nce upon a time there were three little pigs who lived with their mother in a little cottage. Now, as their mother was very poor, the three little pigs decided to go out into the world and seek their fortunes.

The first little pig set off down the road. After a time, he came upon a man carrying a big bundle of straw. "Hello, sir," said the first little pig. "Please sell me that straw so that I can make myself a house." So the man sold the little pig his bundle of straw, and the little pig made himself a cozy house of straw.

No sooner was the house finished than along came a great, big, bad wolf who knocked on the door and cried:

"Little pig! Little pig!
Let me in! Let me in!
Or I'll huff and I'll puff
And I'll blow your house down!"

The little pig replied:

"Oh, no!
I won't let you in.
Not by the hair
Of my chinny-chin-chin!"

And so the wolf huffed and he puffed and he blew down the little pig's house of straw. And the little pig had to run as fast as his feet would carry him or the wolf would have eaten him up!

Shortly afterward, the second little pig set off down the road. Soon he came upon a man carrying a large bundle of sticks. "Hello, sir," said the little pig. "Will you please sell me your sticks so that I can make myself a house?" So the man sold the little pig his bundle of sticks, and the little pig made himself a cozy house of sticks.

No sooner was his house finished when along came the great, big, bad wolf who knocked on the door and cried:

"Little pig! Little pig!
Let me in! Let me in!
Or I'll huff and I'll puff
And I'll blow your house down!"

The second little pig replied:

"Oh, no!
I won't let you in.
Not by the hair
Of my chinny-chin-chin!"

So the wolf huffed and he puffed and he blew down the little pig's house of sticks. Then the little pig had to run like anything or the wolf would have gobbled him up!

Next, the third little pig set off down the road. Soon he came upon a man carrying a big load of bricks. "Hello there, sir," cried the little pig. "Will you sell me your load of bricks so that I can make a house?" So the man sold the bricks to the little pig, and the little pig built himself a cozy brick house.

But no sooner was the third house finished when along came the great, big, bad wolf, and he knocked at the door and cried:

"Little pig! Little pig!
Let me in! Let me in!
Or I'll huff and I'll puff
And I'll blow your house down!"

And the third little pig replied:

"Oh, no!
I won't let you in.
Not by the hair
Of my chinny-chin-chin!"

So the wolf huffed and he puffed and he puffed and he huffed. But no matter how hard he blew, he couldn't blow down the house of bricks!

However, the great, big, bad wolf was not about to give up so easily. He climbed up onto the roof and poked his nose down the chimney.

"I am just poking my nose inside," said the wolf.

"As you wish," replied the little pig.

"And now I am just poking my ears inside," said the wolf, for he did not want the little pig to get frightened and run away.

"As you like," replied the little pig.

"And now I am just putting my paws inside!"

"All right," said the little pig.

"And now I am just putting my tail inside!" said the wolf, climbing down the chimney.

But just then the great, big, bad wolf gave a terrible howl and scrambled back up the chimney as quickly as he could. You see, the clever little pig had put a great big kettle of water on to boil in the fireplace.

And that was the last any of the three little pigs ever saw of the great, big, bad wolf.

Little Red Riding Hood

Once there was a little girl who was so pretty and sweet that she was adored by everyone who met her. Her grandmother loved her best of all and doted on her. Once she made the girl a little red velvet cape with a hood. The child liked it so well that she would wear no other. And that was how she came to be called Little Red Riding Hood.

One day her mother said to her, "Little Red Riding Hood, come take this basket of cakes and butter to your grandmother. She's been quite ill, and they will do her good. Go as quickly as you can. And be sure not to stray from the path or you might get lost in the woods!"

Little Red Riding Hood promised to do as she was told. She skipped down the path with the basket under her arm and headed for her grandmother's on the other side of the woods.

She had not gone far when she met a wolf. Little Red Riding Hood did not know what a wicked creature he was, so she was not at all frightened. "Good morning!" she said.

"And a good morning to you," replied the wolf. "Where are you going in such a hurry?"

"Oh," said Little Red Riding Hood, "I'm taking this basket of cakes to my sick grandmother who lives on the other side of the woods."

"How nice," the wolf said. And as he was feeling very hungry, he thought to himself, "Little Red Riding Hood would make a tasty meal, and her grandmother, too! I must see if I can manage to eat them both!"

So he walked beside Little Red Riding Hood, and after a while he said, "Tell me, Red Riding Hood, why are you walking so quickly? Can't you see how beautiful the woods are this morning? Listen! How the birds are singing! And look at all the pretty flowers!"

Little Red Riding Hood stopped to look around. It truly was a lovely morning. Sunbeams were dancing among the trees, and the flowers were gently bowing their heads in the breeze. "How happy my grandmother would be if I brought her a bunch of flowers!" the child thought. "Besides, it's so early, I can pick them and still get there before too long."

Forgetting what her mother had told her, Little Red Riding Hood left the path and ran into the woods to

gather flowers. She did not mean to be gone long, but every time she pulled a flower, she saw a prettier one farther on. And so on she went, deeper into the forest and farther from the path.

Meanwhile the wolf ran straight to grandmother's house and knocked on the door.

"Who's there?" the grandmother asked.

"It's me," squeaked the wolf, "Little Red Riding Hood. I've brought you a basket full of good things to eat. Open the door!"

"Just come in," the grandmother called back. "The door's open. I'm too weak to get up!"

The wolf pushed open the door, ran upstairs to grandmother's bedroom, and gobbled her up in a single bite! He quickly put on her nightgown and her nightcap and jumped into bed, pulling the covers over himself. He lay quietly waiting for Little Red Riding Hood to come.

Only after Little Red Riding Hood had picked so many flowers that she could not possibly carry one more, did she remember that she was supposed to be at grandmother's house. And so she ran all the way there.

When she arrived, she was surprised to find that the door was wide open. "Hello, Grandmother!" she called. But there was no answer. So she went inside and climbed upstairs to her grandmother's bedroom. As Little Red Riding Hood approached the bed, she thought to herself how strange her grandmother looked.

"Oh, Grandmother," cried Little Red Riding Hood, "what big ears you have!"

"All the better to hear you with, my dear," said the wolf.

"But Grandmother, what big eyes you have!"

"All the better to see you with, my dear!"

"But Grandmother, what big hands you have!"

"All the better to hug you with, my dear!

"But Grandmother," said Little Red Riding Hood, "what big teeth you have!"

"All the better to eat you with!" said the wolf. And as soon as the words were out of his mouth, the wolf sprang out of bed and swallowed Little Red Riding Hood in a single gulp!

By now the wolf was so full, he could hardly walk. He climbed back into bed and fell into a deep sleep.

A short while later, a hunter came walking by the cottage. When he saw the door open, he said to himself, "That's odd. I'd better make sure the old woman is all right!" So he went in and up the stairs and came upon the wolf asleep in the grandmother's bed.

"So I've caught you at last, you old rascal!" the hunter whispered, and he raised his gun to shoot. But then he thought, "The wolf may have eaten the old woman and perhaps there is still time to save her." So he took out a knife and quickly cut open the wolf's stomach while the beast was asleep. Little Red Riding Hood popped out. "Oh, thank you!" she cried. "It was so dark in the wolf's stomach, and I was so frightened!" Then her grandmother came tumbling out. She was alive, too.

The hunter and Little Red Riding Hood fetched some stones and placed them in the wolf's stomach before they sewed it up again. When the wolf woke up, he tried to run away, but the stones were so heavy that he fell down dead.

Then Little Red Riding Hood, her grandmother, and the brave hunter sat down and shared the cakes and butter. Soon Little Red Riding Hood's grandmother was feeling well again. As for Little Red Riding Hood, she had learned her lesson. "I will never again listen to strangers who tell me to stray from the path and go into the woods when Mother has told me not to!" she said to herself. And she never did!

Aesop's Fables

The Fox
and the Crow

A crow who had stolen a piece of cheese was flying to the top of a tall tree to enjoy her prize when a fox spotted her. "If I am clever and handle this right," the fox thought, "I will have that nice piece of cheese for my supper!" So he sat himself under the tree and began to speak to the crow in the politest way he could.

"How well you are looking today, Mistress Crow!" the fox began. "Your wings are so shiny and black! Indeed, you look most noble sitting there like that. I only wish I could hear you sing, for I have never heard your voice, though I'm sure it is as beautiful as the rest of you!"

The vain crow was so delighted to hear such flattery that she flapped her wings and bobbed her head up and down. She was especially thrilled that the fox called her voice "beautiful," for she had often been told that her caw sounded rather raspy.

Thinking to impress the fox with her wonderful voice, she opened her beak wide. "Caw! Caw!" she sang, and down fell the piece of cheese, right into the fox's open jaws!

As he walked away licking his lips, he called up to the crow, "Remember that flatterers are never to be trusted, and that lesson is well worth the loss of your cheese."

And so the poor crow learned that flatterers are never to be trusted!

The Ant
and the Grasshopper

One cold and windy autumn day, an ant was busily storing away the wheat and barley she had gathered over the summer to feed herself during the long, hard winter. As she was working, a grasshopper came limping by, half-dead from hunger and shaking with cold.

"Oh, please, good ant," the grasshopper cried when he saw her. "Please give me a little of your wheat and barley to keep me from starving!"

The ant looked the grasshopper over. "What were you doing all summer long while I was busy gathering grain?" she asked him.

"Oh," the grasshopper replied, "I was not being lazy. I sang and chirped all day long!"

"Well, my good friend," the ant said sternly as she locked her storeroom door, "since you sang all summer, you can surely dance all winter!"

And so the grasshopper learned the bitter lesson that one must always prepare today for the needs of tomorrow.

The Fox
and the Grapes

One day a fox was walking along, feeling very hungry and thirsty. At last, he came upon a sunny vineyard. "Ah," he thought, "some nice juicy grapes would be just the thing for me!" Although there were many tempting bunches of grapes hanging from the vines, they were all too high for him to reach. He jumped as high as he could, snapping at the nearest bunches, but he missed them. He tried again and again. But no matter how hard he tried, he could not reach even a single delicious grape.

At last, angry and worn out, he skulked away, muttering to himself, "I never wanted those grapes anyway. I'm sure they're sour and most unpleasant tasting! Why, I wouldn't eat them even if they were given to me!"

Now, by this simple story of the fox and the grapes we may observe that animals (and people, too) find it easy to scorn what they cannot have.

The Tortoise
and the Hare

———— ✦ ————

There was once a hare who was always making fun of a certain tortoise because he was so slow. Whenever the tortoise was out walking, the hare would spring up ahead of him. "Hurry up, you slowpoke!" he would shout. Or, "Are you sure you're really moving? Maybe you're not going anywhere and don't even know it!" Then the hare would laugh and laugh. The poor tortoise tried not to pay attention to him. But, finally, one day he'd had enough. Before he knew what he was doing, he had challenged the hare to a race.

The hare thought this was the funniest thing he had ever heard. "You?" he said. Then he laughed so hard he almost fell over. "You must be joking. I'll run circles around *you*!"

"Never mind your boasting," the tortoise replied. "Let's just get on with the race."

All the animals of the forest set the course. The fox was chosen to be the judge because of his sharp eyesight, and at his bark, the race began. Almost before you could say "Let's go!" the hare sprang down the path and disappeared from sight. Meanwhile, the tortoise inched along at his usual plodding pace.

After a time, the hare grew tired. "I'll just stop here and wait for the tortoise to show up," he said to himself, flopping down on the grass. He waited a long time. At last, he began to get sleepy. "Perhaps I'll just take a quick nap," he thought. "Then I can finish the race late in the afternoon when it gets cooler." So he closed his eyes, and soon he was fast asleep.

Meanwhile, the tortoise kept plodding along. He passed the hare lying asleep in the soft grass, and on and on he went until he was only a few feet from the finish line. Just then the hare woke with a start, but it was too late to save the race. By the time he arrived at the finish line the other animals were already gathered around the winner: the slow tortoise, who had gotten there first.

And so from the story of the tortoise and the hare we can learn that the one who is slow and steady wins in the end.

Grimm's
Fairy Tales

Cinderella

Once upon a time there lived a rich man who, after the death of his first wife, married the proudest, most disagreeable woman imaginable. His second wife was a widow and had two daughters who were just as unpleasant as she. The man also had a daughter from his first marriage. She was good-hearted and very beautiful, which made her stepmother and stepsisters jealous, and they began to mistreat the girl terribly.

The girl was now made to work from dawn to dusk—cooking, cleaning, and doing all the other household chores. Her fine silk and satin dresses were taken away, and she was given only a tattered gray smock to wear. She was no longer allowed to sleep in a proper bed either. Instead, she was made to sleep on the hearth among the cinders, and because of this, her stepsisters gave her the name Cinderella.

One day it was announced that the king was to give a great ball that would last for three days. All the young ladies in the kingdom were to be invited, for his son, the prince, wished to choose one of them to be his bride. The king's messenger brought three invitations, but the cruel stepsisters told him there were only two young ladies in the household.

As the night of the ball approached, Cinderella's stepsisters were beside themselves with excitement and could speak of nothing else. Now Cinderella was kept twice as busy as before. Her stepsisters ordered her to sew their gowns for the ball and to embroider their best petticoats and to polish the diamond buckles on their shoes.

At last, the day of the ball arrived. All day long Cinderella was kept running to and fro as her stepsisters shouted orders at her. "Cinderella, iron my red velvet dress at once!" cried one. "You must curl my hair!" ordered the other. "Fetch my pearl broach!" said the first. "Polish my ruby bracelet," said the other. Poor Cinderella hardly had a moment to catch her breath. Yet she was so good-hearted that she did all they asked without complaining.

As evening neared, however, Cinderella could not help from saying, "Ah, how I wish I were going to the ball!" Her stepsisters burst into peals of laughter. "You?" they said. "Whatever can you be thinking of? How can you go to the ball? And what would you wear? Your tattered gray smock?" And then they laughed even harder. Cinderella said nothing.

At last, her stepsisters were ready to leave. Cinderella saw them off and stood at the door, staring after their carriage. After it was out of sight, she sat by the hearth and wept as though her heart would break.

She was sobbing so hard that she did not see the strange old woman who suddenly appeared in the doorway. Indeed, she did not know that anyone was there until the woman came up beside her and said, "Tell me, Cinderella, why are you crying?"

"Oh," she sighed, "it's only that I wish . . . I wish . . ."

"You wish you could go to the ball, is that it?" said the old woman. Cinderella nodded.

"And so you shall," the woman told her, for this woman was Cinderella's fairy godmother, and she had come to make the girl's wishes come true. "Dry your tears and listen to me closely," the fairy godmother said. "First, you must fetch the finest pumpkin you can find from the garden. Bring it to me, and then you will see what you will see."

Cinderella did as she was told, and her fairy godmother waved a magic wand over the pumpkin. Instantly, it was transformed into a solid gold coach.

"Now we will go and look in the mousetrap," her fairy godmother said, "and see what we can find there." Six lively gray mice were inside the trap. As Cinderella watched, her fairy godmother tapped each one with her magic wand. In the twinkling of an eye, the six mice became fine gray dappled horses. And a fat rat that was found in the pantry was soon transformed into a jolly coachman with the finest whiskers you have ever seen. Then the fairy godmother told Cinderella to fetch six frogs from the lily pond. With the wave of her wand they became six fine footmen dressed in suits of green.

Cinderella was overjoyed, but then she looked at her clothes, and her face fell, for she was still wearing her old gray smock. "But how can I go to the ball dressed like this?" she asked quietly.

"Do not worry," her fairy godmother replied with a smile. She touched Cinderella with her magic wand. When the girl looked again, she saw that she was dressed in a beautiful gown woven of silver and gold and studded with precious jewels. The fairy godmother then pulled from her pocket a pair of the finest, daintiest glass slippers. Cinderella slipped them on.

"Now, my dear, you are ready to go to the ball," her fairy godmother said. "But you must be sure to leave the ball before the clock strikes twelve, for at that time, my spell will be broken, and your gold coach will again be a pumpkin; your horses, mice; your coachman, the fat rat from the trap; and your footmen, frogs from the lily pond. And your beautiful gown will once more be only a tattered gray smock."

Cinderella promised to do as her fairy godmother had told her, and then she set off for the ball.

When the girl entered the great ballroom, she looked so beautiful that everyone fell silent and stared at her in amazement. "She must be a princess from a faraway land," they all whispered. Even her stepsisters, who did not recognize Cinderella, were full of admiration for the beautiful woman. They paid her many compliments and studied her gown to see how to have one like it made for themselves.

The prince, too, could not take his eyes off the beautiful stranger and would not leave her side. He asked Cinderella to dance every dance and insisted that she sit beside him at dinner. Cinderella had never been so happy, and the night passed as in a beautiful dream.

Cinderella was so overwhelmed with happiness that she quite forgot her fairy godmother's warning and only remembered when the clock had almost finished striking midnight. She leaped to her feet with a cry and dashed from the palace as quickly as she could.

No sooner had she run down the steps and reached the palace gates than her coach became a pumpkin. The beautiful horses were once again mice, and the coachman changed back into a rat. And instead of her elegant gown, she wore only her old rags.

The prince chased after Cinderella, but he could not catch up with her. In her haste Cinderella lost one of her glass slippers on the palace steps. The prince found it and carefully picked it up. It was the loveliest, most delicate slipper he had ever seen. He carried it inside and showed it to his father. "I will marry the girl whose foot fits this slipper," he told the king, "and no other shall ever be my bride."

Cinderella ran home and had just settled herself among the cinders when her stepsisters came home. Pretending she had been sleeping, she asked them about the ball. "Oh, Cinderella," they replied. "You cannot imagine what a beautiful princess came there! Her coach was made all of gold, and her gown was so very splendid!" Cinderella listened quietly. But she could not help smiling when her stepsisters said, "The prince seemed very taken with the strange princess. He danced every dance with her."

"Ah," said Cinderella. "The princess must have been very lovely! How I should have liked to have seen her."

"Yes," said her stepsisters, a little jealously. "She was very fashionable, indeed. But at the stroke of midnight she suddenly disappeared. After she was gone, the prince seemed to lose all interest in the ball! He found her shoe and swore to try it on every maiden in the kingdom until he finds her."

The next day, the king sent out his servants to try the glass slipper on all the ladies in the kingdom. Princesses and duchesses and great ladies all tried on the tiny slipper, but it did not fit one of them. At last, the king's servants arrived at Cinderella's house. Her stepsisters were over-joyed, for they had often been told that their feet were exceptionally small and dainty. But no matter how they pushed and pulled and prodded and poked, they could not get so much as a toe or a heel into the glass slipper! Then, Cinderella, who had been watching, said, "May I please try on the slipper, too?" Her stepsisters rolled their eyes. "You?" they said. "You, who wear rags and sleep among the cinders! How can you possibly imagine that the slipper would fit you?"

The king's servant, who had noticed that the girl was uncommonly pretty, said that it was only fair that she be allowed to try it on, too. So he asked Cinderella to sit down and extend her foot. The glass slipper slipped on as easily as if it had been made for her.

Then, to everyone's amazement, Cinderella took the matching slipper from her pocket. At that moment, unbeknownst to everyone but Cinderella, the fairy godmother appeared in the corner of the room. With a wave of her magic wand, she changed Cinderella's old gray rags into a gown even lovelier than the other one. Now her stepsisters saw that Cinderella was truly the beautiful princess from the ball. Falling to their knees, they begged her pardon for how they had mistreated her. And Cinderella, who was as good as she was kind, willingly forgave them both.

Then she was taken to the prince, who thought her even more wonderful than before. They were married that very day and lived happily ever after.

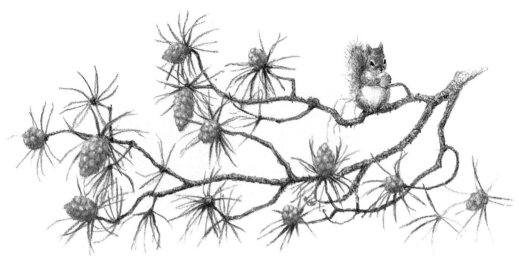

Hansel and Gretel

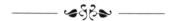

Once upon a time, at the edge of a great forest, there lived
a poor woodcutter with his second wife and the two children
from his first marriage—a boy named Hansel and a girl
named Gretel. A famine fell across the land and times grew hard. Soon
the woodcutter and his family were going hungry. No matter how hard
he thought, the poor man could not think of any way to get enough food
for all of them. One night as he lay awake, he turned to his wife and said,
"What will become of us? How can I earn enough to feed my family?"

"Listen to me, husband," his wife replied. "Tomorrow you must take
the children deep into the forest. There we will build a great fire and give
each of them one last piece of bread. Then we will go about our work
and leave them behind. They will never find their way home, and we will
be rid of them forever."

"I cannot do that!" the husband cried. "How could I abandon my
own dear children in the forest? The wild beasts will surely find them and
tear them to pieces!"

"As you wish," his wife answered. "But if you don't do it, all four of us will surely die of hunger." And she gave him no peace until at last he said, "Very well. I'll do as you wish. But all the same, I pity my poor children."

Hansel and Gretel, who had been kept awake by their hunger, heard their stepmother's words. Gretel began to cry bitterly.

"Don't worry, Gretel," her brother told her. "I will think of a way to save us."

As soon as their parents had gone to sleep, Hansel slipped from his bed, put on his jacket, and stole outside. The moon was shining brightly on the pebbles in front of the house. They gleamed like silver pennies. Hansel bent down and filled his pockets with them. Then he tiptoed back inside. "Don't worry, dear Gretel," he whispered. "Everything will be all right." Then he crept into bed and fell fast asleep.

Early the next morning, before the sun had risen, the stepmother came in to wake the two children. "Get up, you lazybones! We have work to do," she said. "Today we must go into the forest and gather wood."

She gave each of them a small piece of bread, saying, "Here is your lunch. But don't eat it all at once, for that's all you'll get today." Gretel put Hansel's piece under her apron, for his pockets were full of pebbles. Then they all set out into the forest.

After they had gone a little way, Hansel turned around and looked back at the house. Then he stopped and did so again and again.

"Hurry up!" their father called to him. "Why are you dragging behind?"

"Oh, Father, I am just looking at my little white kitten who is sitting on the roof and telling me good-bye," Hansel replied.

"Don't be stupid," his stepmother scolded him. "That isn't your kitten. That's only the morning sun shining on the rooftop."

But Hansel wasn't really looking at his kitten. Each time he turned, he took a pebble from his pocket and dropped it on the path.

When they were deep in the forest their father stopped and said,

"Now gather wood, children, for I'm going to make a big fire to keep you warm." Hansel and Gretel gathered a big pile of twigs and branches. Soon an enormous fire was blazing.

"Lie down beside the fire and rest, children," their stepmother told them. "We are going into the forest to chop more wood. When we're done, we'll come back and fetch you."

So Hansel and Gretel sat beside the fire and ate their pieces of bread. They were not afraid because they thought they heard their father's axe in the distance, but it was really only a dead tree limb knocking against a tree trunk in the wind. After a time their eyelids became heavy, and before long they were fast asleep.

When they woke up, it was night, and the sky was pitch black. Gretel began to cry. "We will never get out of the forest now!" she sobbed. Hansel comforted her. "Wait until the moon rises," he said. "Then you'll see how we can get home again."

When the moon rose, Hansel took his sister's hand. Then they followed the shiny, silvery pebbles on the path all the way home.

They arrived there at daybreak and knocked on the door. When their stepmother answered, she cried, "You bad children, why did you sleep so long in the forest? We thought you'd never come home." But their father was happy to see them, for in his heart he had not wanted to leave them alone in the great forest.

But before long, the woodcutter's cupboards were empty again, and everyone was hungry. "We can't go on like this," his wife said one night. "We must get rid of the children. This time we must take them so deep into the forest, they'll never find their way home!"

The woodcutter argued. "I would rather share my last bit of bread with my children than leave them in the forest," he said. But his wife nagged him so much that at last he agreed.

Hansel and Gretel overheard their stepmother's words. After his parents were asleep, Hansel tried to slip outside to gather more pebbles. But

this time, his stepmother had locked the door. Still, he tried to comfort his sister. "Don't cry, Gretel," he said. "Somehow we will find our way home."

Their stepmother woke them early the next morning. Giving them each a piece of bread that was even smaller than what they had had the last time, she told them they must go into the forest.

Hansel crumbled the bread in his pocket and turned back again and again to scatter the crumbs on the ground.

"Come on!" his father called to him. "What are you doing back there?"

"I am only looking at my little pigeon who is sitting on the roof and telling me good-bye," Hansel replied.

"Don't be stupid!" his stepmother said. "That's not your pigeon. It's only the morning sun shining on the chimney."

This time, their stepmother led them far away into the darkest part of the forest. Once again, their father made a fire, and their stepmother told the children to lie down beside it and rest. Then she and her husband went off into the woods. At noon, Gretel shared her piece of bread with her brother. Then the two children dropped off to sleep.

When they awoke, the sky was pitch black. Gretel started to cry, but Hansel said, "Don't worry, little sister. Wait only until the moon rises. Then we will be able to see the crumbs that I scattered and follow them home."

But when the silver moon rose, there were no crumbs to be seen anywhere. The birds had flown down and eaten every last one.

"We'll still get home somehow," Hansel told his sister. They walked all night and the next day from sunrise to sunset, but try as they might they could not find a way out of the forest.

They were growing very hungry because they could find nothing to eat save a few berries. When they were too tired to walk any farther, they laid down under a tree and fell asleep. When they awoke it was light again.

It was the third morning since they had left their father's house. They began to walk again, but they were so weak that they knew if they did not find food soon they would surely die.

At noon they saw a snow-white bird perched on a branch above their heads. The bird sang so beautifully, the children stopped to listen. When its song was finished, the bird fluttered its wings and flew just in front of them. They followed it until they came to a little house.

The pretty white bird perched on the roof, and as Hansel and Gretel drew closer, they saw that the house was made all of gingerbread and trimmed with raisins, nuts, and jellies. The windows were clear sugar candy, and the roof was made of almond cake.

"Let us eat, little sister," Hansel cried, "and have a good meal. I'll have a piece of the roof, and you can have some of the window—that's sure to be sweet and tasty." So Hansel broke off a piece of the almond cake roof while Gretel nibbled on a windowpane.

Suddenly a voice screeched from inside:

*"Nibble, nibble, little mouse,
Who's that nibbling at my house?"*

The children replied:

*"It is just the wind on high,
We, the children of the sky."*

And they kept right on eating, for they were very hungry. The roof tasted so good Hansel broke off a large piece of it. Gretel knocked out a big round windowpane and sat down and munched on it contentedly.

Suddenly the door of the house flew open, and out came an old, old woman, supporting herself on a cane. Hansel and Gretel were so frightened they started to run away. But the old woman called to them, "Wait, dear children, come back! Come in and stay with me a while. I won't do you any harm." Then she took them by the hand and led them inside.

She sat them down at her table and fed them milk and sugar pancakes and apples and nuts. Then she took them upstairs, where there were two beautiful beds with snow-white linen sheets. As Hansel and Gretel crawled into bed, they thought they were in heaven.

But the old woman was only pretending to be kind and good. She was really a wicked witch who lured children to her gingerbread house and then roasted them and ate them. After Hansel and Gretel had fallen fast asleep, she rubbed her hands together and said, "These children can never escape me now!"

The next morning, the witch woke up early and went to fetch the children. They looked so lovely with their round, rosy cheeks that she couldn't help smiling. "They will make me a very tasty meal!" she cackled. She seized Hansel with her bony hand. She pulled him off to a little cage and locked him inside. He screamed and struggled, but it did no good.

Then she shook Gretel awake. "Get up, you lazy creature!" she shrieked. "Fetch me water so I can cook something good for your brother.

He's outside in my cage, and when he's nice and fat, I'm going to eat him up."

Gretel began to cry, but her tears were for nothing. She had to do as the witch told her.

Now Hansel was fed only the finest meals—roast chicken and beef and boiled potatoes and all the bread he could eat. Every morning, bright and early, the witch crept out to the cage. "Put out your finger so I can see if you're fat enough yet," she would say. But clever Hansel only stuck out a little bone. As the witch was almost blind, she couldn't tell the difference. So she decided Hansel must be fed more so he would become nice and fat.

After a month had passed and Hansel remained as thin as ever, the witch grew impatient. One day she said to Gretel, "I am tired of waiting. Whether Hansel is fat or thin, I'm going to roast him and eat him tomorrow morning."

Gretel wept bitterly. "If only the wild beasts of the forest had eaten us," she said to herself. "At least then my brother and I would have died together."

The next morning, the witch told Gretel to light the oven fire. "I'll soon roast Hansel," the witch said, "but first we will bake some bread. I've already kneaded the dough. Just crawl inside the oven for me and see if it's hot enough." Then she pushed Gretel toward the oven door. Inside the hot flames sputtered.

The old witch meant to close the door as soon as Gretel was inside, for she wished to eat her, too. But Gretel guessed what the witch was planning, so she said, "But I don't know how to climb inside!"

"Don't be so stupid," the witch shrieked. "Why, the door is big enough for me to get in myself!" She stuck her head in the oven, and as she did so, Gretel quickly shoved her inside. Then she slammed the iron door and bolted it shut. The witch screamed horribly, but Gretel didn't open the door until the witch was dead.

Then Gretel ran outside to Hansel and unlocked his cage. "Oh, brother," she cried, throwing her arms around him. "The wicked witch is dead, and we are saved!"

Hansel flew from his prison like a bird set free from its cage. Then, as there was nothing to be afraid of anymore, the two children went hand in hand into the witch's house. There they found chests of pearls and diamonds and other precious jewels.

Hansel filled his pockets with them. "These are better than pebbles," he told Gretel. And so she, too, filled her apron with them. "Now we must find our way home," Hansel said, "and leave this great forest."

The two children walked and walked all day.

At last, the forest began to look familiar. Then the children glimpsed their father's cottage in the distance. They started to run. They ran all the way to the door and rushed inside. There, they found their father sitting by the fire, and they flung their arms around him and held him as if they would never let go.

The woodcutter had not had a happy moment since he had abandoned his children in the deep, dark forest. His wife had since died, as well. The poor man wept with joy when he saw that Hansel and Gretel had come back to him.

Then Gretel emptied her apron of the jewels. Hansel also emptied his pockets, so that pearls, diamonds, sapphires, and rubies skittered all over the room. Wherever they looked jewels gleamed and glittered. Now they were rich and all their troubles were over. They all lived happily ever after.

Rapunzel

T here once lived a man and his wife who longed very much to have a child. At last it seemed that their wish was about to be granted.

A window at the back of their house overlooked a garden full of the most beautiful flowers, fruits, and vegetables. The garden was completely surrounded by a high stone wall. No one dared go into the garden, for it was said to belong to a very powerful and wicked witch.

Now, one day, as the woman looked out over this garden, she caught sight of a bed of fresh, green, leafy rapunzel. The rapunzel looked so delicious her mouth began to water, and she longed with all her heart to eat some. Day by day her longing grew until she knew no peace. At last, her husband noticed how weak and pale she had become and asked her what was wrong. "Oh," the woman replied, "if I do not get some of that rapunzel from the garden behind our house I fear I shall die."

Her husband, who loved her very much, decided that he must get her some of the rapunzel no matter what the cost. That night he crept over the great stone wall. Then he hastily gathered a handful of the rapunzel and took it to his wife. She made a salad of it and quickly devoured it. But the rapunzel tasted so delicious that her longing for it only grew stronger. She begged her husband to fetch her more. And so, once again, the man climbed over the high wall.

He was just bending down to gather the rapunzel when a voice above him shrieked, "Thief! How dare you climb into my garden and steal my rapunzel? You will pay for this with your life."

Looking up, the terrified man saw the angry witch towering over him. He fell to his knees and begged her for mercy. "I only did it for my wife, who is with child," he said. "She glimpsed your rapunzel from our window and longed so much to eat some that I was afraid she would die unless I got it for her."

When she heard this, the witch grew calmer. "Very well," she said. "I will spare your life, and you may take as much of my rapunzel as you wish on one condition. You must give me the baby your wife is about to bear. I can promise you the child will come to no harm, for I will give it every care."

Not knowing what else to do, the man agreed. As soon as the baby was born the witch appeared, named the child Rapunzel, and took the baby away with her.

Rapunzel grew up to be the most beautiful child in all the land. She had sparkling eyes, rosy cheeks, and golden hair so long it fell in ringlets past her feet, forming a long train of gold behind her. Rapunzel was the only living creature the old witch had ever loved. She guarded the child jealously, and when the girl was twelve years old the old witch decided to shut her away from the world altogether. She took Rapunzel to a high tower deep in the forest. This tower had neither a door nor a staircase, but only one tiny window at the very top. Whenever the old witch wanted to visit, she would stand below the window and call up:

"Rapunzel, Rapunzel, let down your hair!"

Then the girl would unpin her long braids of shiny golden hair and, winding them twice around the window hook, let them fall all the way down to the ground. The witch would then climb up to see her beloved Rapunzel.

Several years passed this way. Then one day a prince came riding through the forest. He heard a girl singing, and her voice was so sad and beautiful that he stopped to listen. It was Rapunzel, who often passed the lonely hours by singing to herself. The prince followed the sound of her voice until he reached the tower where Rapunzel was imprisoned.

Eager to see the singer, the prince looked for a door or a stairway, but there was none to be found. At last he gave up and got on his horse and rode home again. But Rapunzel's singing had so moved him that every day he rode to the forest to hear her sing.

One day as the prince stood behind a tree listening, the witch came along and called up:

"Rapunzel, Rapunzel, let down your hair!"

The prince watched as Rapunzel let fall her long, shimmering, golden braids and the witch climbed up them. The very next day at sunset, the prince rode to the tower. Standing just under the window, he cried:

"Rapunzel, Rapunzel, let down your hair!"

The girl threw down her long braids, and up climbed the prince.

At first, Rapunzel was very frightened of the prince, for she had never before seen a man. But the prince spoke gently to her and soon calmed her fears. He told her how beautiful her singing was and how deeply it had touched his heart. The prince's voice and manners were so much sweeter than those of the old witch that soon Rapunzel began to fall in love with him.

He came to visit her every day, making sure to come at sunset when the witch was never around. Then one day he asked her to be his wife and come away with him to his castle. Rapunzel looked at the young, handsome prince. "He is kind and good," she thought. "And he is so much nicer than the old witch." And so she laid her hand in his and said, "Dear prince, I will gladly be your wife and go away with you. But first I must find a way to escape this tower. Each time you visit me, pray bring a skein of silk with you. That way I will be able to weave myself a ladder and leave this wretched tower forever."

And so each evening the prince came, bearing silken thread with him. The witch knew nothing of it, but one day, when the ladder was almost finished, Rapunzel forgot herself and said, "Tell me, Granny, why does it take you so long to climb up here? The prince is up in a flash!"

The witch was furious. "Oh, you wicked girl," she cried. "I have locked you away from all the world. And still you have managed to betray me!" She seized Rapunzel's long braids in one hand, and with the other she picked up a pair of heavy iron scissors. With a great snip she cut off the girl's long golden braids. Then she took Rapunzel away to a bleak desert place where the poor girl was to live in great sorrow and misery.

When Rapunzel was gone, the witch returned to the tower, and picking up the braids, she wrapped them around the window hook and waited. After a time, the prince appeared and called up:

"Rapunzel, Rapunzel, let down your hair!"

At that the witch let down the long, golden braids. The prince climbed up them as always. But instead of his beloved Rapunzel, he found only the old witch. She glared at him spitefully and cackled, "Your beautiful bird has flown her nest, and the cat's got her! Now the cat's going to scratch out your eyes, and you will never see your Rapunzel again!"

With that the witch sprang at the prince, and, in his despair, he leaped from the tower. Although he escaped with his life, he landed in a bed of sharp thorns, and both his eyes were put out.

Blind and broken-hearted, he wandered through the forest for several long years, scarcely knowing or caring where he was. Then, by chance, he wandered into the desert place where Rapunzel was living. He heard a voice singing in the distance, and it sounded beautiful and familiar. He

stumbled toward it, and as he drew nearer, Rapunzel recognized him. Weeping bitterly, she fell into his arms. As she did so, her tears fell on his blinded eyes and his sight grew clear again.

The prince discovered then that he was looking into the eyes of his own beloved Rapunzel. Then he saw that there were two children beside her—twins, a boy and a girl. They were his own children, and Rapunzel had been trying to raise them alone in the barren desert. Now, the prince had nothing more to wish for, and taking Rapunzel's hand, he led her and their children back to his kingdom, where they all lived in peace and happiness for many long years. And as for the unhappy witch, no one knows, for she was never heard of again.

The Frog Prince

In the days when wishes came true, there lived a king who had three daughters. They were all beautiful, but the youngest was so lovely that the sun himself, who had seen everything, was filled with wonder every time he shone on her face.

The king lived in a castle next to a great, dark forest. In the forest under an old oak tree, there was a deep, cool well. Whenever it was hot, the youngest princess sat beside this well. There she amused herself by playing with a pretty gold ball, passing the hours by throwing it into the air and catching it.

One day, the gold ball fell out of reach and into the well. The princess leaned over the edge and looked down. The well was very deep—so deep she could hardly see the bottom. Surely her ball was lost forever! The princess began to cry.

Then she heard a voice calling her. "What's the matter, lovely princess? Why are you crying so pitifully?" it asked.

The princess looked up to see who was speaking. She was surprised to see a frog sitting on the side of the well. "Oh," she said, "I am crying because I lost my gold ball in the well."

"Don't cry," the frog replied. "I can fetch your ball. But what will you give me if I get it back for you?"

"Whatever you wish, dear frog," said the princess, for the ball was her favorite plaything. "I will give you my fine clothes, my jewels, even the gold crown I wear on my head!"

The frog shook his head. "I have no use for your clothes or jewels or even your gold crown," he said. "But if you will love me and be my friend and let me sit beside you at your gold table and eat from your little gold plate and drink from your little gold cup and sleep in your little bed— well, if you promise all that, then I will get back your gold ball."

"Yes, yes," the princess said quickly, "whatever you like." The frog was surely talking nonsense, she thought. How could a frog who sat in the water all day, croaking and catching flies, possibly live among people? With this in mind, she gave her promise.

The frog dived into the deep well. Soon he came paddling up to the surface with the gold ball in his mouth. He hopped out of the well and dropped the ball on the grass before the princess. Delighted to have her beautiful toy again, she picked it up and ran as fast as she could.

"Wait for me," called the frog. "You promised to be my friend and take me home with you. Wait! You're going too fast! I can't keep up." But the princess would not stop. She would not even turn around. Instead, she ran all the way home and quickly forgot the frog.

The next day as the princess was sitting at dinner with her father and all the court and eating from her little gold plate and drinking from her little gold cup, she heard something crawling up the marble steps. *Plip, plot, plip, plop,* it went.

Then there was a knocking at the door.

"Oh, king's youngest daughter, remember your promise and let me in!"

The princess ran to the door to find out who was calling. But when she saw who it was, she slammed the door and returned to the table.

"My daughter," the king said, "what is wrong? Why are you frightened? Is there a giant at the door who's come to carry you away?"

"Oh, no!" the youngest princess replied, "just a horrible, ugly frog!"

"And what does this horrible, ugly frog want from you?" asked the king.

"Oh, Father, yesterday as I was playing beside the well in the forest, my gold ball fell into the water. I cried so much that the frog came to see what was wrong. He said he'd get the ball back for me, if I promised to let him be my friend. But I never thought he would actually leave the well. And now, he's come."

There was a knocking at the door again, and a voice called:

"Oh, king's youngest daughter, let me in.
Don't you remember what you promised—
Yesterday by the cool well water?"

The king turned to the princess. "Whatever you promised, you must honor," he said.

So the princess let the frog in. Hopping slowly and leaving a trail of wet footprints behind him, he followed the princess to her chair. Then he looked up at her and said, "Lift me up beside you."

The princess made a face, but the king ordered her to obey. Then the frog asked the princess to lift him onto the table. Then he said, "Oh, princess, please push your gold plate closer so that I can eat from it, too!" The princess did as the frog asked, but everyone could see she didn't want to. The frog seemed to enjoy the meal, but the princess could eat no more than a bite.

When the meal was over, the frog turned to the princess and said, "Now that I've eaten my fill, I'm feeling quite tired. Please carry me to your bedroom, and let me sleep beside you in your little bed."

The princess burst into tears. "I won't have that awful, cold, wet frog in my nice, clean bed," she sobbed. But the king sternly told her, "If someone helps you when you are in need, you must repay your debt." So the princess reluctantly picked up the frog, carried him to her room, and set him in the corner.

But the frog crawled over to the bed as the princess lay down. "I'm tired," he croaked, "and I'd like to sleep just like you. Pick me up and set me on the pillow beside you."

The princess did as he asked, though she was not at all happy about it. The frog slept on her pillow all night long. When the sun rose, he leaped off the pillow and hopped out of the room, down the stairs, and out the door.

"Thank goodness!" the princess thought to herself. "I won't be bothered with that dreadful frog anymore."

But the next night, as she was sitting down at the table, there came again a knocking at the door. Once more, the frog appeared and asked to eat from her little gold plate and drink from her little gold cup. That night the frog slept on the pillow beside her. The night after that the same thing happened, and no matter how much she cried, the poor princess could not convince her father to put a stop to the frog's visits.

However, on the third morning when she awoke, the princess saw to her amazement that instead of the ugly frog, a handsome young prince stood gazing down at her with a warm smile.

The prince then told the princess that he had been put under a spell by a wicked witch. She had changed him into a frog, and he was doomed to stay in that form until a princess took him from the well and let him sleep in her bed for three nights. "You have freed me from my enchantment," the prince said tenderly. "Now I wish to marry you and take you to my father's kingdom, where I will love you and take care of you for as long as we both shall live."

The princess gave her consent, and together they went to the king and told him what had happened. Their marriage was celebrated that very day, and they both lived together in great happiness for many years.

The Bremen Town Musicians

————— ⋅⋦⋧⋅ —————

There was once a man who owned a donkey. For many years this donkey had cheerfully carried the man's sacks of grain to the mill. But now the donkey was too old and weak to work. The man told himself it cost too much to feed this old donkey, who couldn't even carry his grain to the mill anymore. "I'll have to get rid of him," he thought.

But the donkey guessed what was on his master's mind and decided to run away. He had heard that Bremen was a fine musical town, so, not knowing what else to do, he decided to go there and become a town musician.

He had been on the road a while when he came upon an old hound dog lying across the path and panting as if he had been running for many miles.

"Why are you panting like that, old hound?" asked the donkey.

"Oh," wheezed the dog, "I am old and can no longer hunt as I used to. My master planned to get rid of me, so I ran away. But now I don't know what to do!"

"Why don't you come with me?" said the donkey. "I'm on my way to Bremen to be a town musician! I'll tell you what, I'll play guitar and you can be my drummer."

The old hound immediately agreed, and together the two friends continued on their way. Soon, they came upon a cat sitting by the side of the road and pulling a long face.

"What's the matter with you?" asked the donkey. "You look as gloomy as a month of rainy days!"

"What have I got to be glad about?" sighed the cat. "I am old and my teeth are blunt. Nowadays I'd rather sit by the fire and purr than chase mice. My mistress decided to drown me. I got wind of her plan and ran away, but now I don't know how I'll get along."

"Come with us to Bremen!" cried the donkey. "We're going to be town musicians there, and I know what a fine singer you are!"

The cat liked this idea, and so the three friends went on together. After a while, they came to a farmyard. A cock was sitting on the gate, crowing as loudly as he could. "Why are you singing so loudly, old rooster?" asked the donkey. "You're making enough noise to split my eardrums!"

"Ah," replied the cock sadly. "My mistress has guests coming tomorrow, and she told the cook to make me into a stew. I'm to have my head chopped off tonight, so I'm crowing with all my might while I still can!"

"That's no good," said the donkey. "Why don't you come with us instead? We're on our way to Bremen to be town musicians. Your voice is certainly strong and clear, and I'm sure we could make fine music together!"

The cock quickly said yes, and so the four friends set out. But Bremen was too far to reach in a day. As the sun set, the animals came to a forest and decided to look for a place to spend the night. They spotted a spark of light in the distance, so they set out in that direction. As they approached the light it grew bigger and brighter until they reached a house that was all lit up inside.

The donkey, who was the tallest, went to the window and peered in. It was then he realized that the house belonged to a gang of robbers.

"What do you see, old nag?" asked the cock.

"A table spread with plenty of food and drink," replied the donkey. "And there are robbers sitting around it, enjoying their feast!"

"Robbers!" sighed the cock. "That's too bad. I'd enjoy a good meal right now!"

"Yes," agreed the donkey. "If only we could find a way to get inside."

So the animals discussed how they might chase the robbers out of the house. At last, they came up with a plan.

The donkey laid his front hooves on the windowsill. Then the hound dog leaped up on his back, the cat climbed on top of the dog, and the cock flew up and perched on the cat's head. At the donkey's signal, they all began to make music together.

The donkey brayed, and the dog barked. The cat meowed, and the cock crowed. They made such a horrible noise that all the windows in the house rattled, and, with cries of terror, the robbers fled into the forest.

After the robbers were gone, the four companions went inside and ate and drank enough to last them a month. When they were done, they all began to yawn. The donkey put out the light, and each animal chose the bed where he or she would be most comfortable.

The donkey stretched out on a pile of hay; the dog lay down behind the door; the cat curled up in front of the fire; and the cock perched on the beam of the roof. As it had been a long day, the four friends soon fell fast asleep. The robbers were watching, and when they saw the lights in the house go out, they began to regret having left. "We should never have let ourselves be scared off so easily," said the robbers' chief. He ordered one of the men to go back to the house and have a look around.

When the man reached the house, he found it quiet and dark. He went to the kitchen to get a light. Mistaking the cat's glowing eyes for coals, he held a match up to them. But the cat was in no mood to play. Spitting and scratching, she sprang at him. With a howl of terror, the robber ran for the back door. There the dog jumped up and bit him hard in the leg. Then, as the man raced across the yard past the pile of straw, the donkey gave him a good kick in the ribs. All this commotion woke up the cock, who began crowing with all his might, "Cock-a-doodle-doo!"

The robber ran as fast as he could back to his chief. "That house is fearsome!" he cried. "In the kitchen there's a wicked witch with fiery eyes who spit at me and clawed my face. And behind the door there's a man with a big knife who stabbed me in the leg! In the yard there's a big black monster who almost struck me dead with a club! And on the roof is a judge who cried, 'Bring that villain to me! Bring that villain to me!' I'm lucky I managed to escape with my life!"

When they heard that, the robbers decided never to go near the house again. But the four friends liked it so much that they stayed on. And for all I know they are still there today!

Snow White

One winter day, when snowflakes were falling, a queen sat at her open bedroom window sewing a tapestry on a frame made of black ebony. She accidentally pricked her finger with the needle, and three drops of blood fell upon the snow. The red drops looked so beautiful against the white snow that she said, "I wish I might have a child as white as snow, as red as blood, and as black as ebony." A year later, her wish came true: The queen gave birth to a daughter whose skin was white as snow and whose cheeks were red as blood and whose hair was black as ebony. The queen named the child Snow White.

But the queen died, and a year passed before the king took a second wife. This new queen was very beautiful, but she was also very proud. She could not bear to think that anyone might be as

beautiful as she. Now, this queen's most prized possession was a magic mirror. Every day she stepped in front of it to look at herself and say:

"Mirror, mirror on the wall,
Who is the fairest of them all?"

And the mirror always replied:

"Fair Queen, you are the fairest of them all."

These words made the proud queen very happy, for she knew the mirror would speak only the truth.

As time passed, Snow White grew up. Every day the girl became more beautiful. One morning when the queen stepped in front of her mirror and asked:

"Mirror, mirror on the wall,
Who is the fairest of them all?"

The mirror replied:

"Queen you are very fair, 'tis true,
But Snow White is a thousand times fairer than you."

When the queen heard that, she turned pale with rage and envy. From that moment on, she could not think of Snow White without feeling a bitter pang in her heart. Day by day her hatred grew until it gave her no peace.

At last, she called her huntsman to her and said, "Take the child deep into the forest, for I never want to see her again. Kill her and bring me her heart so I will know that you have done as I commanded."

The huntsman led Snow White deep into the forest. But when he drew his knife, she began to cry. "I will run away into the forest," she pleaded. "I promise I will never come home again. Please spare me my life!"

She was so innocent that the huntsman could not help but take pity on her, and he told her to run away. "It will not be long before the wild beasts devour her," he thought, "but at least she will not die from my hand."

The huntsman killed a wild boar, cut out its heart, and took it back to the queen. The wicked woman ate it, rejoicing that Snow White was dead.

Meanwhile, Snow White found herself alone in the great, dark, snowy forest. She stared up at the branches on the trees and wondered

what would become of her. As night began to fall, she grew afraid and ran through the forest, over sharp stones and past thorny brambles. Wild beasts sprang at her, but she came to no harm.

At last, she spied lights shining through the trees, and following them, she came upon a tiny cottage.

Inside, everything was unusually small and wonderfully clean and neat. There was a little long table covered with a clean white cloth. It was set with seven little plates, spoons, knives, and cups. Against one wall stood seven little beds all in a row covered with snow-white sheets.

Snow White was very hungry and thirsty. So she ate one bite of bread from each plate and took one sip of wine from each cup, for she did not want to take everything from one setting. Then, wearily, she lay down on one of the beds and fell fast asleep.

Later that night, the owners of the cottage came marching in. They were seven dwarves who spent their days digging in the mountains for gold. They saw at once that someone had been in their cottage. And there she was—asleep on one of their beds!

"How beautiful she is!" they all cried at once. They were so touched by the child's beauty that they could not bring themselves to wake her.

The next day when Snow White awoke, she saw the seven dwarves standing around her bed. At first she was frightened, but they greeted her kindly.

"What is your name?" one of them asked.

"Snow White," she replied.

The dwarves asked her how she came to be in their cottage. She told them how her stepmother had ordered the huntsman to take her into the forest and kill her and how he had spared her her life and how she had run away into the woods.

When the dwarves heard all this they said, "If you wish, you may stay with us and keep our house. You can cook, make the beds, and wash our dishes. And if you keep everything neat and clean, we will take good care of you."

"Oh, I would like that." Snow White smiled.

So every morning the seven dwarves went off to the mountains to dig for gold, and Snow White waved good-bye to them from the cottage door. When the dwarves returned each evening, Snow White had cleaned the cottage and fixed a wonderful supper.

Since Snow White spent her days alone in the cottage, the dwarves warned her to beware of her stepmother.

"Be careful and do not let anyone in!" they told her. "Your stepmother will soon find out where you are and come after you."

Believing that she had eaten Snow White's heart, the wicked queen had not bothered to look into her magic mirror. But at that very moment she decided to step in front of it and ask:

"*Mirror, mirror on the wall,*
Who is the fairest of them all?"

And the mirror replied:

"*Queen, you are very fair, 'tis true,*
But over the mountains and through the woods,
In the cottage where the seven dwarves stay,
Snow White is a thousand times more fair."

When she heard that the queen was livid. Her mirror would never lie to her. She knew that the huntsman had deceived her and Snow White was still alive. Late into the night she schemed how she might kill the child so that she would once again be the most beautiful in the land.

At last she came up with a plan. She smeared her face with brown paint and dressed herself in the clothes of an old peddler. Diguised this way, she headed out over the mountains and through the forest to the cottage of the seven dwarves.

"Fine wares for sale!" she cried beneath the cottage window until Snow White peered out.

"Good day, my good woman," Snow White said. "What do you have?"

"Laces of all colors," murmured the wicked queen. "Have a look!" She held out a brightly colored silk lace.

"Surely I can let in this old peddler," Snow White thought. She opened the door and took the pretty lace.

"Ah, come here and let me lace you properly!" said the queen.

Snow White obediently turned around to let the peddler tie the lace in her belt. The queen laced her up so quickly and so tightly that Snow White could not breathe, and she fell to the ground in a faint.

"Now it is over for you, my pretty one," the queen sneered and hurried back to her palace.

When the seven dwarves returned that evening, they found their beautiful Snow White lying still and pale on the floor. When they lifted her up, they could see that her belt had been laced too tightly. Quickly, they undid the lace, and little by little, Snow White began to breathe again. When she was able to speak, she told the dwarves what had happened.

"That peddler was your wicked stepmother," they told her. "Now you know you must be even more on guard and let no one into the cottage when we are away."

As soon as the wicked queen was home, she rushed to her mirror and asked:

"Mirror, mirror, on the wall,
Who is the fairest of them all?"

And the mirror replied:

"Queen, you are very fair, 'tis true,
But over the mountains and through the woods,
In the cottage where the seven dwarves are,
Snow White is a thousand times fairer than you."

When the queen heard that her heart beat as if it would burst, for she knew that Snow White was still alive.

All that night and the next day, the queen thought long and hard to devise a better plan to kill her rival. She finally decided to make a poisoned comb. Disguising herself as another old peddler, she set out for the seven dwarves' cottage. When she arrived, she knocked on the door and cried out, "Beautiful combs for sale!"

Snow White peered out the window. "You had better go on your way, good woman," she said. "I may not let anyone in."

"But you can at least look, can't you?" the wicked queen said, holding out the poisoned comb. It glinted so prettily in the light that Snow White couldn't help herself. She opened the door and let the woman in.

When the girl had agreed to buy the comb, the peddler said, "Now let me place the comb properly in your hair!" Snow White, suspecting nothing, bent her head over. But as soon as the comb was in her hair, the poison began to work, and she fell down as if dead.

"Now your beauty is nothing!" cried the wicked queen. And with that she returned to her palace.

The sun was setting when the seven dwarves came marching home. Horrified, they found Snow White lying as if dead on the cottage floor. They knew at once it was the wicked queen's doing. Terribly afraid, they examined her carefully and found the poisoned comb. They pulled it from her hair, and within moments Snow White began to breathe again. When she told them what had happened, they warned her even more strongly that she must be carfeul and not open the door to *anyone*.

Meanwhile, back in her chamber, the wicked queen stepped before her magic mirror and said:

"Mirror, mirror on the wall,
Who is the fairest of them all?"

And it replied as it had before:

"Queen, you are very fair, 'tis true,
But over the mountains and through the woods,
At the cottage where the seven dwarves dwell,
Snow White is a thousand times more fair than you."

When she heard that, the queen couldn't contain her rage. Shaking violently and stamping her foot, she swore that she would find a way to kill Snow White.

This time she went into a secret room in the heart of the palace, and there she prepared a poisoned apple. This rosy apple looked so fresh that whoever saw it could not help but crave a bite. When her work was done, the wicked queen disguised herself as an old farm woman and set out once more for the cottage of the seven dwarves.

When she arrived at the cottage, Snow White said to her firmly, "You had best be on your way, my good woman. The seven dwarves have forbidden me to let anyone in."

"But you need not open the door," the wicked queen told her. "I only wish to sell my apples. Here, let me give you one."

"No, thank you," Snow White replied. "I dare not take it."

"What are you afraid of?" asked the wicked queen. "You don't think I'd poison you, do you? Look, I'll share the apple with you. I'll have one half, and you, the other." However, the wicked queen had made the apple with such skill that only one half was poisoned.

When Snow White saw the farm woman bite into the beautiful apple, her mouth began to water. She put out her hand and accepted the poisoned half. But no sooner had she taken the first bite than she fell to the ground dead.

The wicked queen began to laugh. "White as snow, red as blood, and black as ebony," she crooned. "This time even the seven dwarves cannot save you."

At home again before her mirror, she asked:

"Mirror, mirror, on the wall,
Who is the fairest of them all?"

And the mirror replied:

"Queen, there is no one as fair as you."

The queen smiled and was at peace—as much at peace as a jealous heart can ever be.

When the dwarves came home that evening, they found Snow White dead and cold. They held a mirror to her lips, but no breath fogged the glass. They lifted her up and searched her for a poisoned object. They unlaced her stays and combed her hair and even washed her face with water and wine, but nothing they did would bring her back to life. She was truly dead.

At last, the dwarves lay Snow White out on a bier of sweet wood. For three days, they stood around her bier and wept. When it was time to bury her they could not bring themselves to lay her in the cold ground. She still looked as if she were alive, with her skin white as snow and her cheeks red as blood and her hair black as ebony.

Instead the seven dwarves made beautiful Snow White a coffin of glass so that she could still be seen by all the living creatures of the world. When it was finished, they gently laid her inside. Across the top they engraved her name in gold letters and wrote that she was the daughter of a king. Then they carried the glass coffin up to the mountain, and one of them always kept watch over it.

For many years, Snow White lay in the glass coffin. Yet strangely, she remained as fresh and lovely as if she were still alive.

One day a king's son chanced upon the seven dwarves' cottage. Looking up the mountain, he saw the glass coffin glittering in the sun, and he rode up to have a look at it. When he saw the beautiful Snow White and

read the gold letters, he went to the dwarves and said, "Please let me have the maiden in the glass coffin. I will give you whatever you ask for her."

But the dwarves refused. "We would not give her up for all the gold and jewels in the world," they said.

"Then give her to me as a present," pleaded the prince, "for I cannot live without looking on her. I promise to love her and cherish her as the person dearest in the world to me." When he said that, the seven dwarves took pity on him and agreed that he could take Snow White.

The prince ordered his servants to lift the coffin onto their shoulders and carry it to his palace. On the way, one of the servants tripped over a thorny bramble and let the coffin fall to the ground, where it broke open. At that, the piece of poisoned apple flew out of Snow White's throat, and with a start, she opened her eyes.

"Where am I?" she gasped, sitting up.

The prince replied with joy, "You are with me, and here I wish you to stay forever." He told her what had happened and who he was. Then he asked her to be his wife and come and live with him at his father's castle.

Snow White, who had fallen in love with the kind prince on sight, gave him her hand.

Their wedding feast was soon announced, and the wicked stepmother was invited to the celebration. Little did she know that it was Snow White's wedding she was dressing for in her finest gown of gold and silver. Before she left, she stepped in front of her magic mirror and asked:

> "Mirror, mirror on the wall,
> Who is the fairest of them all?"

And the mirror replied:

> "Queen, you are very fair, 'tis true,
> But the young princess is a thousand times fairer than you."

When the wicked queen heard that a chill passed through her. She was terribly afraid. She did not even want to attend the wedding. In the end, she could not stay away. She would have no peace until she had seen this young queen whom her magic mirror had declared most beautiful of all.

When she arrived at the prince's palace, she recognized Snow White at once. As she set eyes on the girl all the hate in her evil heart swelled until, in a fit of passion, it burst, and she fell down dead. With no one to wish them harm in the world, Snow White and her prince lived happily ever after.

Rumpelstiltskin

❧ §❧ ❧

There was once a poor miller who had a very beautiful daughter. One day when the king was hunting nearby, he stopped at the miller's cottage. In order to seem more important, the miller told him that his daughter had the gift of spinning straw into gold.

The king, who had a great love of gold, said, "If your daughter can indeed do as you say, I should like to meet her. Bring her to the castle in the morning, and I will put her to the test."

When the young woman arrived at the castle, the king led her to a large room filled with straw. He gave her a spinning wheel and said, "Get to work, but I warn you, if you haven't spun all this straw into gold by tomorrow morning, you will pay with your life." With that he locked the door, and the woman was left alone.

The miller's daughter didn't know what to do. She didn't have the slightest idea how to spin straw into gold. She thought and thought, and the more she thought, the more frightened she became. Finally she burst into tears.

Suddenly the door flew open, and a strange little man walked in. "Good evening, miller's daughter," he said. "Why are you weeping?"

"Oh," said the miller's daughter, "the king has said I must spin all this straw into gold, and I don't know how. So tomorrow I must die."

"What will you give me if I spin it for you?" asked the little man.

"I will give you the necklace from around my neck," replied the miller's daughter.

So the little man took the necklace, sat down at the spinning wheel, and started spinning. Around and around whirred the wheel, and soon the bobbin was full of shining golden thread. Then the little man filled another bobbin, and another, until all the straw had been spun into gold.

When the sun rose, the king came and unlocked the door. When he saw the gold he was overjoyed. Yet the sight of so much gold made him greedier still. He led the miller's beautiful daughter to a room that was even larger than the first one and piled to the ceiling with straw. Once again, he gave her a spinning wheel and told her to spin all the straw into gold or she would lose her life.

When the king had gone, the miller's daughter began to cry. Once again the door flew open, and the little man appeared before her.

"What will you give me this time if I spin the straw into gold for you?" he asked.

"I will give you the ring from my finger," answered the miller's daughter.

So the little man set to work as quickly and as nimbly as before. And when the rising sun streaked the sky, all the straw had been spun into glittering gold.

The king was beside himself. Yet he hungered for still more gold. So he led the miller's daughter to a third room—larger by far than the other two and completely stuffed with straw. "You must spin all this straw into gold or lose your life," he said. "But if you succeed, I will make you my queen." He was thinking to himself that although she was a poor miller's daughter, he would never find a woman who could bring him more wealth. Then he locked the door and went away.

Almost as soon as the king had gone, the door flew open a third time and the little man came in.

"What will you give me to spin the straw for you one last time?" the man asked.

The young woman began to cry. "I have nothing left to give you," she sobbed.

"Never mind that," said the little man. "Only promise me that if you become queen, you will give me your first child."

Because the miller's daughter could think of nothing else, she agreed. When he had her promise, the little man sat down at the spinning wheel and kept it whirring all night long until every bit of straw had been spun into gold.

The next morning, when the king saw all the gleaming gold, he married the miller's beautiful daughter, and so she became a queen.

A year later she gave birth to a child. The queen was very happy and never gave a thought to the little man or her promise. But one day the door flew open once more, and there he was. "I have come to claim what you promised me," he said.

When she heard that, the queen was petrified. She offered the little man all the treasure in the kingdom if he would only let her keep her child.

But all he would say was, "I'd rather have a living child than all the gold and jewels in the world."

When she heard this, the queen began to weep and lament so bitterly that at last the little man took pity on her and said, "Very well, I will give you three days. If you can guess my name in that time you may keep your child."

All night long the queen lay awake and thought of every name she had ever heard.

When the little man came back the next morning, she began by asking him if his name was Casper or Abelard or Melchior or Balthazar. "No," he said to each one. Then she went on to recite all the names she had ever heard—Michalmus and Adolphus and Ezekiel—and more obscure names still. But after each one, the little man replied, "No. That is not my name."

The second day, the queen sent her servants all across the land. They collected all the outlandish and peculiar names they could find. When

the little man arrived, the queen went through them all. "Is your name Mutton-chops?" she asked. "Bootlace? Or Long-nose?" Each time the little man only answered, "No. That is not my name."

On the third day, one of the queen's servants returned to say that, although he had not been able to find any new names anywhere, he had a strange story to tell her. As he was passing through the forest near a high mountain, where even the fox and the hare say good-night to each other, he had come upon a little cottage. "Out in front a fire was burning," he said, "and a funny little man was hopping up and down around it on one leg, singing:

" 'I'll feast tomorrow, I'll bake today,
On the third, I'll take the queen's child away.
A good thing she knows not who I am.
For Rumpelstiltskin is my name!' "

When the queen heard this, she burst into tears of joy.

Later that morning, the little man presented himself before her and asked, "Tell me, your majesty, what is my name?"

The queen replied, "Why, is your name Henry?"

"No."

"Is your name Krispen?"

"No."

"Could your name be Rumpelstiltskin?"

At the sound of his name, the little man burst into a rage. His eyes flashed, and he gnashed his teeth and shouted, "The Devil told you that! The Devil told you that!" And he stamped his foot so hard it went right through the floor. Then he grabbed his other foot with both hands to pull himself out. But he was so angry, he tore himself in two!

And that was the last the queen ever saw of Rumpelstiltskin!

Mother Goose's
Nursery Rhymes

Humpty Dumpty

Humpty Dumpty sat on a wall,
Humpty Dumpty had a great fall.
All the king's horses and all the king's men,
Couldn't put Humpty Dumpty together again.

There Was
An Old Woman

There was an old woman
who lived in a'shoe,
She had so many children
she didn't know what to do;
She gave them some broth
without any bread;
She whipped them all soundly
and put them to bed.

There Was
A Crooked Man

There was a crooked man,
And he walked a crooked mile,
He found a crooked sixpence
Against a crooked stile;
He bought a crooked cat,
which caught a crooked mouse,
And they all lived together
In a little crooked house.

Hey Diddle, Diddle

Hey diddle, diddle,
The cat and the fiddle,
The cow jumped over the moon;
The little dog laughed
To see such sport
And the dish ran away
with the spoon.

This Little Piggy

This little piggy
 went to market,
This little piggy
 stayed home;

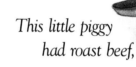

This little piggy
 had roast beef,

This little piggy had none,

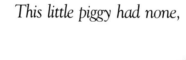

And this little piggy
 cried wee-wee-wee
 all the way home.

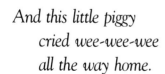

140

Rain, Rain

Rain, rain, go away, Come again another day.

The Lion and
The Unicorn

The lion and the unicorn
Were fighting for the crown;
The lion beat the unicorn,
All about the town.

Some gave them white bread,
And some gave them brown,
Some gave them plum cake
And drummed them
out of town.

Mistress Mary

Mistress Mary, quite contrary,
How does your garden grow?
With silver bells, and cockle shells,
And pretty maids all in a row.

Children's Classics

A Mad Tea-Party

from *ALICE'S ADVENTURES IN WONDERLAND*

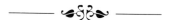

There was a table set out under a tree in front of the house, and the March Hare and the Hatter were having tea at it: a Dormouse was sitting between them, fast asleep, and the other two were using it as a cushion, resting their elbows on it, and talking over its head. "Very uncomfortable for the Dormouse," thought Alice; "only as it's asleep, I suppose it doesn't mind."

The table was a large one, but the three were all crowded together at one corner of it. "No room! No room!" they cried out when they saw Alice coming. "There's *plenty* of room!" said Alice indignantly, and she sat down in a large arm-chair at one end of the table.

"Have some wine," the March Hare said in an encouraging tone.

Alice looked all round the table, but there was nothing on it but tea. "I don't see any wine," she remarked.

"There isn't any," said the March Hare.

"Then it wasn't very civil of you to offer it," said Alice angrily.

"It wasn't very civil of you to sit down without being invited," said the March Hare.

"I didn't know it was *your* table," said Alice: "it's laid for a great many more than three."

"Your hair wants cutting," said the Hatter. He had been looking at Alice for some time with great curiosity, and this was his first speech.

"You should learn not to make personal remarks," Alice said with some severity: "it's very rude."

The Hatter opened his eyes very wide on hearing this; but all he *said* was "Why is a raven like a writing-desk?"

"Come, we shall have some fun now!" thought Alice. "I'm glad they've begun asking riddles—I believe I can guess that," she added aloud.

"Do you mean that you think you can find out the answer to it?" said the March Hare.

"Exactly so," said Alice.

"Then you should say what you mean," the March Hare went on.

"I do," Alice hastily replied; "at least—at least I mean what I say— that's the same thing, you know."

"Not the same thing a bit!" said the Hatter. "Why, you might just as well say that 'I see what I eat' is the same thing as 'I eat what I see'!"

"You might just as well say," added the March Hare, "that 'I like what I get' is the same thing as 'I get what I like'!"

"You might just as well say," added the Dormouse, which seemed to be talking in its sleep, "that 'I breathe when I sleep' is the same thing as 'I sleep when I breathe'!"

"It *is* the same thing with you," said the Hatter, and here the conversation dropped, and the party sat silent for a minute, while Alice thought over all she could remember about ravens and writing-desks, which wasn't much.

The Hatter was the first to break the silence. "What day of the month is it?" he said, turning to Alice: he had taken his watch out of his pocket, and was looking at it uneasily, shaking it every now and then, and holding it to his ear.

Alice considered a little, and then said "The fourth."

"Two days wrong!" sighed the Hatter. "I told you butter wouldn't suit the works!" he added, looking angrily at the March Hare.

"It was the *best* butter," the March Hare meekly replied.

"Yes, but some crumbs must have got in as well," the Hatter grumbled: "you shouldn't have put it in with the bread-knife."

The March Hare took the watch and looked at it gloomily: then he dipped it into his cup of tea, and looked at it again: but he could think of nothing better to say than his first remark, "It was the *best* butter, you know."

Alice had been looking over his shoulder with some curiosity. "What a funny watch!" she remarked. "It tells the day of the month, and doesn't tell what o'clock it is!"

"Why should it?" muttered the Hatter. "Does *your* watch tell you what year it is?"

"Of course not," Alice replied very readily: "but that's because it stays the same year for such a long time together."

"Which is just the case with *mine*," said the Hatter.

Alice felt dreadfully puzzled. The Hatter's remark seemed to her to have no sort of meaning in it, and yet it was certainly English. "I don't quite understand you," she said, as politely as she could.

"The Dormouse is asleep again," said the Hatter, and he poured a little hot tea upon its nose.

The Dormouse shook its head impatiently, and said, without opening its eyes, "Of course, of course: just what I was going to remark myself."

"Have you guessed the riddle yet?" the Hatter said, turning to Alice again.

"No, I give it up," Alice replied. "What's the answer?"

"I haven't the slightest idea," said the Hatter.

"Nor I," said the March Hare.

Alice sighed wearily. "I think you might do something better with the time," she said, "than wasting it in asking riddles that have no answers."

"If you knew Time as well as I do," said the Hatter, "you wouldn't talk about wasting *it*. It's *him*."

"I don't know what you mean," said Alice.

"Of course you don't!" the Hatter said, tossing his head contemptuously. "I dare say you never even spoke to Time!"

"Perhaps not," Alice cautiously replied; "but I know I have to beat time when I learn music."

"Ah! That accounts for it," said the Hatter. "He won't stand beating. Now, if you only kept on good terms with him, he'd do almost anything you liked with the clock. For instance, suppose it were nine o'clock in the morning, just time to begin lessons: you'd only have to whisper a hint to Time, and round goes the clock in a twinkling! Half-past one, time for dinner!"

("I only wish it was," the March Hare said to itself in a whisper.)

"That would be grand, certainly," said Alice thoughtfully; "but then—I shouldn't be hungry for it, you know."

"Not at first, perhaps," said the Hatter: "but you could keep it to half-past one as long as you liked."

"Is that the way *you* manage?" Alice asked.

The Hatter shook his head mournfully. "Not I!" he replied. "We quarreled last March—just before *he* went mad, you know—" (pointing with his teaspoon at the March Hare) "—it was at the great concert given by the Queen of Hearts, and I had to sing

> '*Twinkle, twinkle, little bat!*
> *How I wonder what you're at!*'

You know the song, perhaps?"

"I've heard something like it," said Alice.

"It goes on, you know," the Hatter continued, "in this way:—

> '*Up above the world you fly,*
> *Like a tea-tray in the sky.*
> *Twinkle, twinkle—*' "

Here the Dormouse shook itself, and began singing in its sleep "*Twinkle, twinkle, twinkle, twinkle—*" and went on so long that they had to pinch it to make it stop.

"Well, I'd hardly finished the first verse," said the Hatter, "when the Queen bawled out 'He's murdering the time! Off with his head!' "

"How dreadfully savage!" exclaimed Alice.

"And ever since that," the Hatter went on in a mournful tone, "he won't do a thing I ask! It's always six o'clock now."

A bright idea came into Alice's head. "Is that the reason so many tea-things are put out here?" she asked.

"Yes, that's it," said the Hatter with a sigh: "it's always tea-time, and we've no time to wash the things between whiles."

"Then you keep moving round, I suppose?" said Alice.

"Exactly so," said the Hatter: "as the things get used up."

"But what happens when you come to the beginning again?" Alice ventured to ask.

"Suppose we change the subject," the March Hare interrupted, yawning. "I'm getting tired of this. I vote the young lady tells us a story."

"I'm afraid I don't know one," said Alice, rather alarmed at the proposal.

"Then the Dormouse shall!" they both cried. "Wake up, Dormouse!" And they pinched it on both sides at once.

The Dormouse slowly opened his eyes. "I wasn't asleep," it said in a hoarse, feeble voice, "I heard every word you fellows were saying."

"Tell us a story!" said the March Hare.

"Yes, please do!" pleaded Alice.

"And be quick about it," added the Hatter, "or you'll be asleep again before it's done."

"Once upon a time there were three little sisters," the Dormouse began in a great hurry; "and their names were Elsie, Lacie, and Tillie; and they lived at the bottom of a well—"

"What did they live on?" said Alice, who always took a great interest in questions of eating and drinking.

"They lived on treacle," said the Dormouse, after thinking a minute or two.

"They couldn't have done that, you know," Alice gently remarked. "They'd have been ill."

"So they were," said the Dormouse; "*very* ill."

Alice tried a little to fancy to herself what such an extraordinary way of living would be like, but it puzzled her to much: so she went on: "But why did they live at the bottom of a well?"

"Take some more tea," the March Hare said to Alice, very earnestly.

"I've had nothing yet," Alice replied in an offended tone: "so I can't take more."

"You mean you can't take *less*," said the Hatter: "it's very easy to take *more* than nothing."

"Nobody asked *your* opinion," said Alice.

"Who's making personal remarks now?" the Hatter asked triumphantly.

Alice did not quite know what to say to this: so she helped herself to some tea and bread-and-butter, and then turned to the Dormouse, and repeated her question. "Why did they live at the bottom of a well?"

The Dormouse again took a minute or two to think about it, and then said "It was a treacle-well."

"There's no such thing!" Alice was beginning very angrily, but the Hatter and the March Hare went "Sh! Sh!" and the Dormouse sulkily re-marked "If you can't be civil, you'd better finish the story for yourself."

"No, please go on!" Alice said very humbly. "I won't interrupt you again. I dare say there may be *one*."

"One, indeed!" said the Dormouse indignantly. However, he con-sented to go on. "And so these three little sisters—they were learning to draw, you know—"

"What did they draw?" said Alice, quite forgetting her promise.

"Treacle," said the Dormouse, without considering at all, this time.

"I want a clean cup," interrupted the Hatter: "let's all move one place on."

He moved on as he spoke, and the Dormouse followed him: the March Hare moved into the Dormouse's place, and Alice rather un-willingly took the place of the March Hare. The Hatter was the only one who got any advantage from the change; and Alice was a good deal worse off than before, as the March Hare had just upset the milk-jug into his plate.

Alice did not wish to offend the Dormouse again, so she began very cautiously: "But I don't understand. Where did they draw the treacle from?"

"You can draw water out of a water-well," said the Hatter; "so I should think you could draw treacle out of a treacle-well—eh, stupid?"

"But they were *in* the well," Alice said to the Dormouse, not choosing to notice this last remark.

"Of course they were," said the Dormouse: "well in."

This answer so confused poor Alice, that she let the Dormouse go on for some time without interrupting it.

"They were learning to draw," the Dormouse went on, yawning and rubbing its eyes, for it was getting very sleepy; "and they drew all manner of things—everything that begins with an M—"

"Why with an M?" said Alice.

"Why not?" said the March Hare.

Alice was silent.

The Dormouse had closed its eyes by this time, and was going off into a doze; but, on being pinched by the Hatter, it woke up again with a little shriek, and went on: "—that begins with an M, such as mouse-traps, and the moon, and memory, and muchness—you know you say things are 'much of a muchness'—did you ever see such a thing as a drawing of a muchness!"

"Really, now you ask me," said Alice, very much confused, "I don't think—"

"Then you shouldn't talk," said the Hatter.

This piece of rudeness was more than Alice could bear: she got up in great disgust, and walked off: the Dormouse fell asleep instantly, and neither of the others took the least notice of her going, though she looked back once or twice, half hoping that they would call after her: the last time she saw them, they were trying to put the Dormouse into the teapot.

"At any rate I'll never go *there* again!" said Alice, as she picked her way through the wood. "It's the stupidest tea-party I ever was at in all my life!"

Just as she said this, she noticed that one of the trees had a door leading right into it. "That's very curious!" she thought. "But everything's curious today. I think I may as well go in at once." And in she went.

Once more she found herself in the long hall, and close to the little glass table. "Now, I'll manage better this time," she said to herself, and began by taking the little golden key, and unlocking the door that led into the garden. Then she set to work nibbling at the mushroom (she had kept a piece of it in her pocket) till she was about a foot high: then she walked down the little passage: and *then*—she found herself at last in the beautiful garden, among the bright flower-beds and the cool fountains.

The Cat and the Fox Again

from *PINOCCHIO*

The Fairy with the Blue Hair let Pinocchio wail and howl for a good half hour about his long nose, which had grown so much that he could not turn his head without banging the wall. She only did it to teach him a lesson about the folly of telling lies, the worst habit a boy can have. But when she saw his face all red from despair and his eyes all swollen from crying, she took pity on him. She clapped her hands, and at that signal a large flock of woodpeckers flew in through the window. They perched on Pinocchio's long nose and pecked away at it so hard that in a few moments it was back to its proper size.

"How good you are, dear Fairy!" cried Pinocchio, wiping his eyes.

"Would you like to stay here with me and be my little brother?" asked the Fairy.

"Oh, gladly!" the puppet exclaimed. "But what about my poor father?"

"I have already taken care of that. Your father has been told where you are, and he will be here before nightfall."

"Really?" cried Pinocchio, dancing about with delight. "Let me go and meet him. I can hardly wait to hug my poor old father, who has been through so much for me."

"Go, then, but be careful you don't get lost. Take the path through the forest and you will soon meet up with him."

Pinocchio set off, and when he entered the forest he began running as fast as a deer in order to see his father quicker. But at a certain spot near the Great Oak, he stopped because he thought he heard someone. And he did! Can you guess who he saw coming along the road? Why it was the Fox and the Cat, the same two he had dined with at the Red Lobster Inn just the night before.

"Why, if it isn't our dear Pinocchio!" exclaimed the Fox, throwing both arms around the puppet's neck. "What a surprise to meet you here."

"It's a long story," said Pinocchio, "too long to tell you now. But I will say that after you left me at the inn, I met two thieves on the road."

"Two thieves? Oh, my poor friend! And what did they want?"

"They tried to steal my pieces of gold."

"How wicked!" cried the Fox.

"How *very* wicked," repeated the Cat.

"I got away from them," continued Pinocchio, "but they came after me and caught me and hung me from a branch of that very oak." And Pinocchio pointed to the Greak Oak.

"Did you ever!" exclaimed the Fox indignantly. "What a world we live in, where respectable people can't be safe anymore!"

While they were talking, Pinocchio noticed that one of the Cat's paws was bandaged, and he asked, "What has happened to your paw?"

The Cat seemed confused and did not know how to answer, so the Fox quickly spoke up: "My friend is so modest! He got his foot hurt by trying to help an old wolf. Oh, my friend has such a kind heart!" And with that the Fox wiped away a tear.

Pinocchio was very moved by this story and patted the Cat on the shoulder.

"Where are you off to now?" asked the Fox.

"I'm meeting my father, who should be coming along any moment."

"And your pieces of gold?"

"They are still safe in my pocket—all but the one I spent on our dinners at the Red Lobster, of course."

"Just think, instead of four pieces of gold you could have a thousand by tomorrow—or two! Why don't you take my advice, dear friend, and plant them in the Field of Miracles?"

"Oh, I'm afraid that's impossible today. I will go another time."

"Another time will be too late," said the Fox.

"Why?" asked Pinocchio.

"Because a rich man has just bought this land, and after today no one will be allowed to plant anything on it."

"How far is the Field of Miracles?"

"Only about two miles. Oh, do come with us. We'll be there in half an hour, and you can plant your gold coins at once. Then in just a few minutes you'll be able to harvest your two thousand and return home this evening with your pockets bulging. Will you come along now?"

Pinocchio thought about the advice of the good Fairy and kind old Gepetto and the Talking Cricket. But in the end he did what all silly boys do who just want to please themselves. With a careless toss of his head, he said to the Fox and the Cat, "All right, then, I'm with you!"

And off they went.

When they had walked not merely a half an hour but nearly a half a day, they came to a city called Fools-Trap. Pinocchio saw that the city's streets were full of lice-ridden dogs yawning from hunger, shorn sheep trembling from cold, plucked chickens begging for a grain of corn, and many other pitiful animals as well. Butterflies hobbled about because they had sold their beautiful wings, and peacocks hung their heads in shame because their gold-and-silver tails had been cut off.

And from time to time through this crowd of beggars and forlorn creatures, rolled fine carriages with a fancy Fox sitting inside, or a thieving Magpie, or a preying Vulture.

"Where is the Field of Miracles?" demanded Pinocchio.

"We are almost there," said the Fox.

Sure enough, as soon as they had passed beyond the city walls they found themselves in a deserted field. The Fox declared it was the Field of Miracles, though, I must say, it looked like any other field to me.

"Now," said the Fox, "just get down and dig a little hole with your hands and plant your gold pieces."

Pinocchio did as the Fox told him. He dug a hole, put the four coins in it, then covered the hole again.

"Now, then," said the Fox, "bring a little water from that pond over there and sprinkle it on the spot where you have planted your gold."

Pinocchio went to the pond, and as he had no bucket, he took off one of his shoes, filled it with water, and sprinkled the ground where his coins were planted. Then he asked, "Now what do I do?"

"Nothing else," replied the Fox. "Now you can go away. Come back in twenty minutes, and you will find a little tree sprouting up, with all its branches bearing gold pieces."

The foolish puppet was beside himself with greedy joy. He thanked the Fox and Cat over and over and promised them a present.

"Oh, we don't want anything," they replied. "Our best reward is to have taught you how to get rich without working hard at it. Yes, that is enough for us."

And with these words, they made their farewells to Pinocchio, wished him a fine harvest, and were off.

The Piper at the Gates of Dawn

from *THE WIND IN THE WILLOWS*

The Willow Wren was twittering his thin little song, hidden himself in the dark selvedge of the river bank. Though it was past ten o'clock at night, the sky still clung to and retained some lingering skirts of light from the departed day; and the sullen heats of the torrid afternoon broke up and rolled away at the dispersing touch of the cool fingers of the short midsummer night. Mole lay stretched on the bank, still panting from the stress of the fierce day that had been cloudless from dawn to late sunset, and waited for his friend to return. He had been on the river with some companions, leaving the Water Rat free to keep an engagement of long standing with Otter; and he had come back to find the house dark and deserted, and no sign of Rat, who was doubtless keeping it up late with his old comrade. It was still too hot to think of staying indoors, so he lay on some cool dock leaves, and thought over the past day and its doings, and how very good they all had been.

The Rat's light footfall was presently heard approaching over the parched grass. "O, the blessed coolness!" he said, and sat down, gazing thoughtfully into the river, silent and preoccupied.

"You stayed to supper, of course?" said the Mole presently.

"Simply had to," said the Rat. "They wouldn't hear of my going before. You know how kind they always are. And they made things as jolly for me as ever they could, right up to the moment I left. But I felt a brute all the time, as it was clear to me they were very unhappy, though they tried to hide it. Mole, I'm afraid they're in trouble. Little Portly is missing again; and you know what a lot his father thinks of him, though he never says much about it."

"What, that child?" said the Mole lightly. "Well, suppose he is; why worry about it? He's always straying off and getting lost, and turning up again; he's so adventurous. But no harm ever happens to him. Everybody hereabouts knows him and likes him, just as they do old Otter, and you may be sure some animal or other will come across him and bring him back again all right. Why, we've found him ourselves, miles from home and quite self-possessed and cheerful!"

"Yes; but this time it's more serious," said the Rat gravely. "He's been missing for some days now, and the Otters have hunted everywhere, high and low, without finding the slightest trace. And they've asked every animal, too, for miles around, and no one knows anything about him. Otter's evidently more anxious than he'll admit. I got out of him that young Portly hasn't learned to swim very well yet, and I can see he's thinking of the weir. There's a lot of water coming down still, considering the time of year, and the place always had a fascination for the child. And then there are—well, traps and things—*you* know. Otter's not the fellow to be nervous about any son of his before it's time. And now he *is* nervous. When I left, he came out with me—said he wanted some air, and talked about stretching his legs. But I could see it wasn't that, so I drew him out and pumped him, and got it all from him at last. He was going to spend the night watching by the ford. You know the place where

163

the old fort used to be, in bygone days before they built the bridge?"

"I know it well," said the Mole. "But why should Otter choose to watch there?"

"Well, it seems that it was there he gave Portly his first swimming lesson," continued the Rat. "From that shallow, gravelly spit near the bank. And it was there he used to teach him fishing, and there young Portly caught his first fish, of which he was so very proud. The child loved the spot, and Otter thinks that if he came wandering back from wherever he is—if he *is* anywhere by this time, poor little chap—he might make for the ford he was so fond of; or if he came across it he'd remember it well, and stop there and play, perhaps. So Otter goes there every night and watches—on the chance, you know, just on the chance!"

They were silent for a time, both thinking of the same thing—the lonely, heartsore animal, crouched by the ford, watching and waiting, the long night through—on the chance.

"Well, well," said the Rat presently, "I suppose we ought to be thinking about turning in." But he never offered to move.

"Rat," said the Mole, "I simply can't go and turn in and go to sleep, and *do* nothing, even though there doesn't seem to be anything to be done. We'll get the boat out, and paddle upstream. The moon will be up in an hour or so, and then we will search as well as we can—anyhow, it will be better than going to bed and doing *nothing*."

"Just what I was thinking myself," said the Rat. "It's not the sort of night for bed anyhow; and daybreak is not so very far off, and then we may pick up some news of him from early risers as we go along."

They got the boat out, and the Rat took the sculls, paddling with caution. Out in midstream there was a clear, narrow track that faintly reflected the sky; but wherever shadows fell on the water from bank, bush, or tree, they were as solid to all appearance as the banks themselves, and the Mole had to steer with judgment accordingly. Dark and deserted as it was, the night was full of small noises, song and chatter and rustling, tell-

ing of the busy little population who were up
and about, plying their trades and vocations
through the night till sunshine should fall
on them at last and send them off to
their well-earned repose. The water's
own noises, too, were more apparent
than by day, its gurglings and "cloops"
more unexpected and near at hand;
and constantly they started at what
seemed a sudden clear call from an
actual articulate voice.

The line of the horizon was clear
and hard against the sky, and in one
particular quarter it showed black against
a silvery climbing phosphorescence that
grew and grew. At last, over the rim of the
waiting earth the moon lifted with slow majesty
till it swung clear of the horizon and rode off, free of
moorings; and once more they began to see surfaces—meadows wide-
spread, and quiet gardens; and the river itself from bank to bank, all
softly disclosed, all washed clean of mystery and terror, all radiant again
as by day, but with a difference that was tremendous. Their old haunts
greeted them again in other raiment, as if they had slipped away and put
on this pure new apparel and come quietly back, smiling as they shyly
waited to see if they would be recognized again under it.

Fastening their boat to a willow, the friends landed in this silent, silver kingdom, and patiently explored the hedges, the hollow trees, the
tunnels and their little culverts, the ditches and dry waterways. Embark-
ing again and crossing over, they worked their way up the stream in this
manner, while the moon, serene and detached in a cloudless sky, did
what she could, though so far off, to help them in their quest; till her

hour came and she sank earthwards reluctantly, and left them, and mystery once more held field and river.

Then a change began slowly to declare itself. The horizon became clearer, field and tree came more into sight, and somehow with a different look; the mystery began to drop away from them. A bird piped suddenly, and was still; and a light breeze sprang up and set the reeds and bulrushes rustling. Rat, who was in the stern of the boat, while Mole sculled, sat up suddenly and listened with a passionate intentness. Mole, who with gentle strokes was just keeping the boat moving while he scanned the banks with care, looked at him with curiosity.

"It's gone!" sighed the Rat, sinking back in his seat again. "So beautiful and strange and new! Since it was to end so soon, I almost wish I had never heard it. For it has roused a longing in me that is pain, and nothing seems worthwhile but just to hear that sound once more and go on listening to it forever. No! There it is again!" he cried, alert once more. Entranced, he was silent for a long space, spellbound.

"Now it passes on and I begin to lose it," he said presently. "O, Mole! the beauty of it! The merry bubble and joy, the thin, clear, happy call of the distant piping! Such music I never dreamed of, and the call in it is stronger even than the music is sweet! Row on, Mole, row! For the music and the call must be for us."

The Mole, greatly wondering, obeyed. "I hear nothing myself," he said, "but the wind playing in the reeds and rushes and osiers."

The Rat never answered, if indeed he heard. Rapt, transported, trembling, he was possessed in all his senses by this new divine thing that caught up his helpless soul and swung and dandled it, a powerless but happy infant, in a strong sustaining grasp.

In silence Mole rowed steadily and soon they came to a point where the river divided, a long backwater branching off to one side. With a slight movement of his head Rat, who had long dropped the rudder lines, directed the rower to take the backwater. The creeping tide of light gained and gained, and now they could see the color of the flowers that gemmed the water's edge.

"Clearer and nearer still," cried the Rat joyously. "Now you must surely hear it—Ah—at last—I see you do!"

Breathless and transfixed the Mole stopped rowing as the liquid run of that glad piping broke on him like a wave, caught him up, and possessed him utterly. He saw the tears on his comrade's cheeks, and bowed his head and understood. For a space they hung there, brushed by the purple loose-strife that fringed the bank; then the clear imperious summons that marched hand in hand with the intoxicating melody imposed its will on Mole, and mechanically he bent to his oars again. And the light grew steadily stronger, but no birds sang as they were wont to do at the approach of dawn; and but for the heavenly music all was marvelously still.

On either side of them, as they glided onwards, the rich meadow grass seemed that morning of a freshness and a greenness unsurpassable. Never had they noticed the roses so vivid, the willow herb so riotous, the meadowsweet so odorous and pervading. Then the murmur of the approaching weir began to hold the air, and they felt a consciousness that they were nearing the end, whatever it might be, that surely awaited their expedition.

A wide half-circle of foam and glinting lights and shining shoulders of green water, the great weir closed the backwater from bank to bank, troubled all the quiet surface with twirling eddies and floating foam streaks, and deadened all other sounds with its solemn and soothing rumble. In midmost of the stream, embraced in the weir's shimmering arm spread, a small island lay anchored, fringed close with willow and silver birch and alder. Reserved, shy, but full of significance, it hid whatever it might hold behind a veil, keeping it till the hour should come, and, with the hour, those who were called and chosen.

Slowly, but with no doubt or hesitation whatever, and in something of a solemn expectancy, the two animals passed through the broken, tumultuous water and moored their boat at the flowery margin of the island. In silence they landed, and pushed through the blossom and scented herbage and undergrowth that led up to the level ground, till they stood on a little lawn of a marvelous green, set round with Nature's own orchard trees—crab apple, wild cherry, and sloe.

"This is the place of my song-dream, the place the music played to me," whispered the Rat, as if in a trance. "Here, in this holy place, here if anywhere, surely we shall find Him!"

Then suddenly the Mole felt a great Awe fall upon him, an awe that turned his muscles to water, bowed his head, and rooted his feet to the ground. It was no panic terror—indeed he felt wonderfully at peace and happy—but it was an awe that smote and held him and, without seeing, he knew it could only mean that some august Presence was very, very near. With difficulty he turned to look for his friend, and saw him at his side, cowed, stricken, and trembling violently. And still there was utter silence in the populous bird-haunted branches around them; and still the light grew and grew.

Perhaps he would never have dared to raise his eyes, but that, though the piping was now hushed, the call and the summons seemed still dominant and imperious. He might not refuse, were Death himself waiting to strike him instantly, once he had looked with mortal eye on things rightly kept hidden. Trembling he obeyed, and raised his humble head; and then, in that utter clearness of the imminent dawn, while Nature, flushed with fullness of incredible color, seemed to hold her breath for the event, he looked in the very eyes of the Friend and Helper; saw the backward sweep of the curved horns, gleaming in the growing daylight; saw the stern, hooked nose between the kindly eyes that were looking down on them humorously, while the bearded mouth broke into a half-smile at the corners; saw the rippling muscles on the arm that lay across the broad

chest, the long supple hand still holding the panpipes only just fallen away from the parted lips; saw the splendid curves of the shaggy limbs disposed in majestic ease on the sward; saw, last of all, nestling between his very hooves, sleeping soundly in entire peace and contentment, the little, round, podgy, childish form of the baby otter. All this he saw, for one moment breathless and intense, vivid on the morning sky; and still, as he looked, he lived, and still, as he lived, he wondered.

"Rat!" he found breath to whisper, shaking. "Are you afraid?"

"Afraid?" murmured the Rat, his eyes shining with unutterable love. "Afraid! Of *Him?* O, never, never! And yet—and yet—O, Mole, I am afraid!"

Then the two animals, crouching to the earth, bowed their heads and did worship.

Sudden and magnificent, the sun's broad golden disc showed itself over the horizon facing them; and the first rays, shooting across the level water meadows, took the animals full in the eyes and dazzled them. When they were able to look once more, the Vision had vanished, and the air was full of the carol of birds that hailed the dawn.

As they stared blankly, in dumb misery deepening as they slowly realized all they had seen and all they had lost, a capricious little breeze, dancing up from the surface of the water, tossed the aspens, shook the dewy roses, and blew lightly and caressingly in their faces, and with its soft touch came instant oblivion. For this is the last best gift that the kindly demigod is careful to bestow on those to whom he has revealed himself in their helping: the gift of forgetfulness. Lest the awful remembrance should remain and grow, and overshadow mirth and pleasure, and the great haunting memory should spoil all the afterlives of little animals helped out of difficulties, in order that they should be happy and light-hearted as before.

Mole rubbed his eyes and stared at Rat, who was looking about him in a puzzled sort of way. "I beg your pardon; what did you say, Rat?" he asked.

"I think I was only remarking," said the Rat slowly, "that this was the right sort of place and that here, if anywhere, we should find him. And look! Why, there he is, the little fellow!" And with a cry of delight he ran towards the slumbering Portly.

But Mole stood still a moment, held in thought. As one wakened suddenly from a beautiful dream, who struggles to recall it, and can recapture nothing but a dim sense of the beauty of it, the beauty! Till that, too, fades away in its turn, and the dreamer bitterly accepts the hard, cold waking and all its penalties; so Mole, after struggling with his memory for a brief space, shook his head sadly and followed the Rat.

Portly woke up with a joyous squeak, and wriggled with pleasure at the sight of his father's friends, who had played with him so often in past days. In a moment, however, his face grew blank, and he fell to hunting round in a circle with pleading whine. As a child that has fallen happily asleep in its nurse's arms, and wakes to find itself alone and laid in a strange place, and searches corners and cupboards, and runs from room to room, despair growing silently in its heart, even so Portly searched the island and searched, dogged and unwearying, till at last the black moment came for giving it up and sitting down and crying bitterly.

The Mole ran quickly to comfort the little animal; but Rat, lingering, looked long and doubtfully at certain hoof marks deep in the sward.

"Some—great—animal—has been here," he murmured slowly and thoughtfully; and stood musing, musing; his mind strangely stirred.

"Come along Rat!" called the Mole. "Think of poor Otter, waiting up there by the ford!"

Portly had soon been comforted by the promise of a treat—a jaunt on the river in Mr Rat's real boat; and the two animals conducted him to the water's side, placed him securely between them in the bottom of the boat, and paddled off down the backwater. The sun was fully up by now, and

171

hot on them, birds sang lustily and without restraint, and flowers smiled and nodded from either bank, but somehow—so thought the animals—with less of richness and blaze of color than they seemed to remember seeing quite recently somewhere—they wondered where.

The main river reached again, they turned the boat's head upstream, towards the point where they knew their friend was keeping his lonely vigil. As they drew near the familiar ford, the Mole took the boat in to the bank, and they lifted Portly out and set him on his legs on the tow-path, gave him his marching orders and a friendly farewell pat on the back, and shoved out into midstream. They watched the little animal as he waddled along the path contentedly and with importance; watched him till they saw his muzzle suddenly lift and his waddle break into a clumsy amble as he quickened his pace with shrill whines and wriggles of recognition. Looking up the river, they could see the Otter start up, tense and rigid, from out of the shallows where he crouched in dumb patience, and could hear his amazed and joyous bark as he bounded up through the osiers on to the path. Then the Mole, with a strong pull on one oar, swung the boat round and let the full stream bear them down again whither it would, their quest now happily ended.

"I feel strangely tired, Rat," said the Mole, leaning wearily over his oars as the boat drifted. "It's being up all night, you'll say, perhaps; but that's nothing. We do as much half the nights of the week, at this time of the year. No; I feel as if I had been through something very exciting and rather terrible, and it was just over; and yet nothing particular has happened."

"Or something very surprising and splendid and beautiful," murmured the Rat, leaning back and closing his eyes. "I feel just as you do, Mole; simply dead tired, though not body-tired. It's lucky we've got the stream with us, to take us home. Isn't it jolly to feel the sun again, soaking into one's bones! And hark to the wind playing in the reeds!"

"It's like music—faraway music," said the Mole, nodding drowsily.

"So I was thinking," murmured the Rat, dreamful and languid. "Dance music—the lilting sort that runs on without a stop—but with words in it, too—it passes into words and out of them again—I catch them at intervals—then it is dance music once more, and then nothing but the reeds' soft thin whispering."

"You hear better than I," said the Mole sadly. "I cannot catch the words."

"Let me try and give you them," said the Rat softly, his eyes still closed. "Now it is turning into words again—faint but clear—*Lest the awe should dwell—And turn your frolic to fret—You shall look on my power at the helping hour—But then you shall forget!* Now the reeds take it up— *forget, forget,* they sigh, and it dies away in a rustle and a whisper. Then the voice returns—

"*Lest Limbs be reddened and rent—I spring the trap that is set—As I loose the snare you may glimpse me there—For surely you shall forget!* Row nearer, Mole, nearer to the reeds! It is hard to catch, and grows each minute fainter.

"*Helper and healer, I cheer—Small waifs in the woodland wet—Strays I find in it, wounds I bind in it—Bidding them all forget!* Nearer, Mole, nearer! No, it is no good; the song has died away into reed talk."

"But what do the words mean?" asked the wondering Mole.

"That I do not know," said the Rat simply. "I passed them on to you as they reached me. Ah! now they return again, and this time full and clear! This time, at last, it is the real, the unmistakable thing, simple— passionate—perfect—"

"Well, let's have it, then," said the Mole, after he had waited patiently for a few minutes, half dozing in the hot sun.

But no answer came. He looked, and understood the silence. With a smile of much happiness on his face, and something of a listening look still lingering there, the weary Rat was fast asleep.

Toyland

from *THE NUTCRACKER*

———— ❧❦❧ ————

I'm certain, children, that you wouldn't have hesitated for a moment to go with the Nutcracker, who'd proven to be such a good fellow. Marie was all the more inclined to follow him because she knew he was filled with gratitude for all her help. So she said, "Of course I'll go with you, dear Mr. Drosselmeier. But not very far and not for too long. I need to get some rest."

"Then we'll take the shortest route," replied the Nutcracker, "though it's probably the most difficult."

He led Marie to the big old wardrobe. She was surprised to see that it was wide open, with her father's traveling coat hanging right in front. The Nutcracker took hold of the hem and climbed up along the edge of the fox trim until he arrived at a big tassel fastened at the shoulder of the coat. He gave the tassel a tug and a pretty little cedar ladder came down from one of the sleeves.

"Now, Miss Stahlbaum, if you would be so kind as to step up the ladder," said the Nutcracker. And so she did. As soon as she'd gotten as far

up as the neck of the coat, however, a dazzling light poured over her, and she found herself in a sweet-smelling meadow which glittered like millions of beautiful gems.

"This is Candy Meadow," the Nutcracker explained. "Come. Let's go through that gate there."

Marie looked up and saw a lovely gate a few steps away. It seemed at first to be made of white, brown, and raisin-colored marble, but as she drew closer, she realized it was made of baked sugar almonds and raisins. The Nutcracker called it Almond Raisin Gate and pointed out a walkway running along the top of it, where six monkeys in little red suits played trumpets and French horns. The road they were on was made of pieces of multicolored hard candies of every flavor. It led to a forest that was fragrant with the scent of oranges. Beautiful ribbons hung from the trees, and every branch was heavy with gold and silver fruits. A gentle breeze stirred the forest, so the glittering tinsel ribbons rustled like beautiful music, as light danced off the fruit of the swaying branches.

"How very charming!" said Marie, entranced.

"Dear Miss Stahlbaum," said the Nutcracker, "this is Christmas Wood."

"Oh," said Marie, "if only I could stay here a little while. It's *so* lovely."

The Nutcracker clapped his hands, and immediately shepherds and shepherdesses molded of white sugar appeared from a different part of the wood. They brought out a gold reclining chair with a white satin cushion and invited Marie to sit down. As soon as Marie was comfortable, the shepherds and shepherdesses performed a ballet for her and then disappeared back into the forest.

"I apologize for the poor quality of the dance, my dear Miss Stahlbaum," said the Nutcracker. "Our

176

Wind-up Ballet Troupe can only do the same steps over and over again. Let's go on a little farther."

"But I thought it was lovely," said Marie. "Really." She stood up and followed the Nutcracker along a rippling brook. The scent of oranges was even stronger and sweeter here.

"This is Orange Brook," said the Nutcracker. "Its scent is sweet, but the waters of River Lemonade are far more beautiful. Both streams run into the Almond Milk Sea. Come, I'll show you."

As they crested the next hill, Marie heard the sound of rushing water, and, looking down, she saw the large rolling swells of the River Lemonade. A cool freshness blew across her cheeks, gladdening her heart. Nearby was a slow, narrower stream, where children sat on the banks, scooping up the little round fishes that swam in its waters. As Marie approached, she saw the fish were really hazelnuts and that up ahead was a little village, whose golden-brown buildings were decorated with lemon peel and shelled almonds.

"This is Gingertown on the Honey River," said the Nutcracker. "The inhabitants are very good-looking, but they suffer from such painful toothaches that they're usually quite cranky. We'll come back another time."

A short distance away, Marie could see a cluster of houses that seemed to be made of multicolored sheets of glass. The Nutcracker led the way into the town, where a crowd of pleasant little people were busy unloading tiny packages of colored paper and tablets of chocolate from a long line of wagons.

"This is Bonbonville," the Nutcracker said. "Supplies have just arrived from Paperland and the King of Chocolate. These poor citizens have been repeatedly threatened by the Fly Admiral's forces, so they're covering their homes with special-issue sticky sheets from Paperland. But forgive me, Miss Stahlbaum. I won't bore you any longer with the small towns and villages. It's high time you saw the capital."

He proceeded quickly and Marie followed, full of anticipation. A rosy mist began to cover the land around them, giving everything a soft splendor. Marie saw that the mist was reflected in the stream that gurgled alongside them, flowing out toward the horizon, where it widened into a lake with waves of red and silver. On these waters, white swans with collars of gold floated gracefully by, singing to them, while fish which glittered like diamonds danced over the rosy waves.

"Oh, my!" said Marie. "I know what this is. It's the lake Godpapa was going to make for me so that I could play with the swans!"

The Nutcracker smiled scornfully and laughed in a way that Marie had never seen before. "I doubt it," he said. "My uncle could never make a lake like this. You could, Marie, if you wanted to. But let's not worry about that now. It's time to sail over Lake Rosa to the city."

The Capital of Toyland

The Nutcracker clapped his hands and the waves of Lake Rosa grew higher. As Marie watched, a carriage made of precious stones approached, pulled by two dolphins with scales of gold. Then twelve beautiful Nubian boys with headdresses and jackets made of hummingbirds' feathers jumped ashore and led Marie and the Nutcracker into the shell-shaped carriage, which then moved through the water of its own accord. In the wake of the dolphins, water shot up into the air and came down in a sparkling rain that seemed to say in a chorus of tiny voices,

> *Who comes over the rosy sea? Fairy is she.*
> *Fishes and swans, awake and sing. Sparkle and ring.*
> *Here is the fairy we've longed to see,*
> *Coming at last to us over the sea.*
> *Rosy waves dash, bright dolphins speed. Merrily, merrily on!*

But the twelve boys at the back of the car had their own song, and they shook the palm leaves they were holding and stamped their feet and sang:

> *Klapp and klipp, klipp and klapp,*
> *Down and up, up and down.*

"These fellows are quite amusing," said the Nutcracker. "But they'll probably set the whole lake in an uproar, and then where will we be?"

Indeed, they noticed a great confusion of strange voices floating in the water and in the air around them. Marie paid no attention to the feuding songs but continued to gaze at the rosy waters, where she saw the beautiful face of a young girl smiling up at her from every wave.

"Look, Mr. Drosselmeier," she said, pointing into the water. "There's Princess Pirlipat smiling back at me!"

The Nutcracker sighed deeply and said, "That is not Princess Pirlipat, dear Miss Stahlbaum. It's you. That is your own lovely reflection you see in the waves."

Marie, who was terribly embarrassed, instantly shut her eyes and leaned back in her seat. But then the twelve little boys lifted her out of the water carriage and set her down on shore. When she opened her eyes, she found herself in a grove even more beautiful than Christmas Wood. The fruits on the trees were extraordinary and wonderful, and an enticing fragrance surrounded her.

"Ah! Here we are in Sugar Plum Grove, and there's the capital."

Dear reader, how can I begin to describe all the wonderful things Marie saw here, or give you any idea of the magnificence of the city that rose up before her on a flowery plain? The walls and towers shimmered with different colors, and the shapes of the buildings were like nothing Marie had ever seen. Instead of a roof, each house had its own crown, with towers that were exquisitely carved with the most intricate designs. As they passed through the gateway, which was made of macaroons and candied fruits, silver soldiers presented arms in their honor, and a little man in a brocade coat threw his arms around the Nutcracker and said, "Welcome, my prince! Welcome to Candytown!"

Marie wondered why the Nutcracker was called a prince by such a distinguished person. Then she heard a loud, joyous clamor from voices all around her and such laughing and singing that she just had to ask young Drosselmeier what it all meant.

"Oh, it's nothing, dear Miss Stahlbaum," he said. "Candytown is a big city, full of merrymaking. This sort of thing goes on every day. Let's continue on a little farther."

They stopped by the marketplace, where all the houses were round and made of delicately filigreed sugarwork, with balconies one above the other, running all the way up to the top. In the center of the market was a square with a monumental cake shaped like an obelisk in the middle, surrounded by fountains which bubbled over with lemonade and other beverages. Alongside the market footpaths were streams of custard which could be scooped up with a big spoon. But best of all were the delightful townspeople who shouted and laughed and sang—people who came from every nation and walk of life, ladies and gentlemen alike, Greeks, Armenians, Austrians, Chinese, officers, clergymen, and shepherds, all beautifully dressed and having a wonderful time.

The commotion peaked at one particular corner, as the great mogul passed in a carriage carried by four men, with ninety-three noblemen following in attendance along with seven hundred servants. Unfortunately, five hundred memebers of the Fishermen's Guild were having a festival on the opposite corner. So when the great mogul decided to direct his entourage across the street, and *another* procession, for the Glories of Nature, began marching toward the obelisk, "Hail, all hail the magnificent sun!" with a full orchestra in tow, there were just too many people in one place. Consequently, there was pushing and shoving until cries of pain arose from the crowd; for one of the fishermen had accidentally knocked off a Brahmin's head, and the great mogul had nearly been run down by a pudding man! The throng grew wilder and wilder till the man in brocade climbed atop the obelisk and shouted very loudly three times: "Pastrycook! Pastrycook! Pastrycook!"

Immediately there was quiet. Everybody tried to straighten himself as best he could and disentangle the different parades. The Brahmin's head was stuck back on, and people went on celebrating as before.

"Why did that man yell 'Pastrycook,' Mr. Drosselmeier?" asked Marie.

"Dearest Miss Stahlbaum," said the Nutcracker, "here, 'pastrycook' is what we call the power that rules the destiny of these happy people. The mere mention of the name stops everyone from dwelling on earthly matters, such as blows to the head and small injuries and so on, and causes them to consider the nature of man and the course of his ultimate destiny."

They went on to a castle with a hundred shining towers, and Marie couldn't help uttering a cry of admiration as it came into view. Bouquets of violets, narcissus, tulips, and carnations decorated the outside, their rich colors showing off the rose-tinted white walls splendidly. The center dome as well as each one of the pointed towers was sprinkled with thousands of sparkling gold and silver stars.

"And now," announced the Nutcracker, "last but not least, we come to Marzipan Castle!"

Marie noticed that one of the castle's principal towers was missing a roof. Little men on a scaffold of cinnamon sticks were busy replacing it.

"What happened up there?" she asked.

The Nutcracker explained. "Not long ago," he said, "this castle was threatened with total destruction. Sweet Tooth, the giant, bit off the top of that tower and was about to start in on the great dome. The people of Candytown had to give him a whole quarter of the town, not to mention a large slice of Sugar Plum Grove, to keep him from finishing it off."

Soft, beautiful music floated out of the castle, and twelve pages appeared with torches made of clove sticks, lighting up the outside. Each one had a lovely pearl for a head, a body made of emeralds and rubies, and feet of pure gold. After them, four ladies about the size of Marie's Miss Clara approached. They were so exquisitely dressed that Marie felt they could be no less than royal princesses. They embraced the Nutcracker, tears of gladness in their eyes, and cried, "Oh, dearest prince! Beloved brother!"

The Nutcracker wiped away tears of his own, then took Marie by the hand and addressed his sisters from the heart: "This is Miss Marie Stahlbaum, the daughter of a very distinguished doctor. She has saved my life. If she hadn't thrown her slipper at exactly the right moment, and if she hadn't found me a sword, I would be cold in my grave right now, bitten to death by the accursed Mouse King. I ask you, can Princess Pirlipat, princess though she is, compare with Miss Stahlbaum in beauty, goodness, and true virtue? I say emphatically 'No.'"

The ladies cried "No!" in unison and hugged Marie, sobbing and crying out, "Thank you for saving our brother, good Miss Stahlbaum!"

They led Marie and the Nutcracker into the castle, to a hall where the walls were made of sparkling crystal. But what Marie liked best was the furniture. The prettiest little chairs, bureaus, and writing tables, all made of cedar or brazilwood and covered with golden flowers, were placed about the room most elegantly. The princesses made Marie and their brother sit down while they prepared a banquet to welcome them. They

brought out cups and dishes of delicate Japanese procelain, and spoons, knives, forks, graters and stew pots all made of silver and gold. Taking fruits, nuts, and sweets that Marie had never seen before, they squeezed the fruit daintily by hand, grated the spices, and washed the almonds in a way that won Marie's admiration for their skill. She secretly wished that she could assist the princesses in their work and so have helped with these pies herself. Just then, as if reading her mind, one of the Nutcracker's sisters looked up and said, "Good friend, savior of our brother, would you mind pounding some of this sugar candy with us?"

Marie joined them gladly and ground the candy into a sweet paste. The sounds of the work for the banquet blended into a rhythmic song, and the Nutcracker added his voice to it by telling them in great detail about the awful battle he'd fought against the army of the Mouse King. He told of how his troops had let him down, how he had almost been bitten to death, and how Marie had sacrificed several of those dear to her to help him.

Even though Marie was listening carefully, she found it harder and harder to hear the Nutcracker's voice or the sound of her own grinding. They seemed to be getting farther and farther away from her. Then a silvery mist arose in the hall like clouds, and the princesses, the pages, the Nutcracker, and she herself were all floating. There was a buzzing and humming around her that gradually faded away, and she seemed to be ascending up—up—up on waves of silver, rising higher and higher.

"Hook or Me This Time"
from *PETER PAN*

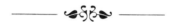

Odd things happen to all of us on our way through life without our noticing for a time that they have happened. Thus, to take an instance, we suddenly discover that we have been deaf in one ear for we don't know how long, but, say, half an hour. Now such an experience had come that night to Peter. When last we saw him he was stealing across the island with one finger to his lips and his dagger at the ready. He had seen the crocodile pass by without noticing anything peculiar about it, but by and by he remembered that it had not been ticking. At first he thought this eerie, but soon he concluded rightly that the clock had run down.

Without giving a thought to what might be the feelings of a fellow-creature thus abruptly deprived of its closest companion, Peter at once considered how he could turn the catastrophe to his own use; and he decided to tick, so that wild beasts should believe he was the crocodile and let him pass unmolested. He ticked superbly, but with one unforeseen result. The crocodile was among those who heard the sound, and it followed him, though whether with the purpose of regaining what it had lost, or merely as a friend under the belief that it was again ticking itself, will never be certainly known, for, like all slaves to a fixed idea, it was a stupid beast.

Peter reached the shore without mishap, and went straight on; his legs encountering the water as if quite unaware that they had entered a new element. Thus many animals pass from land to water, but no other human of whom I know. As he swam he had but one thought: "Hook or me this time." He had ticked so long that he now went on ticking without knowing that he was doing it. Had he known he would have stopped, for to board the brig by the help of the tick, though an ingenious idea, had not occurred to him.

On the contrary, he thought he had scaled her side as noiseless as a mouse; and he was amazed to see the pirates cowering from him, with Hook in their midst as abject as if he had heard the crocodile.

The crocodile! No sooner did Peter remember it than he heard the ticking. At first he thought the sound did come from the crocodile, and he looked behind him swiftly. Then he realized that he was doing it him-self, and in a flash he understood the situation. "How clever of me," he thought at once, and signed to the boys not to burst into applause.

189

It was at this moment that Ed Teynte the quartermaster emerged from the forecastle and came along the deck. Now, reader, time what happened by your watch. Peter struck true and deep. John clapped his hands on the illfated pirate's mouth to stifle the dying groan. He fell forward. Four boys caught him to prevent the thud. Peter gave the signal, and the carrion was cast overboard. There was a splash, and then silence. How long has it taken?

"One!" (Slightly had begun to count.)

None too soon, Peter, every inch of him on tiptoe, vanished into the cabin; for more than one pirate was screwing up his courage to look round. They could hear each other's distressed breathing now, which showed them that the more terrible sound had passed.

"It's gone, captain," Smee said, wiping his spectacles. "All's still again."

Slowly Hook let his head emerge from his ruff, and listened so intently that he could have caught the echo of the tick. There was not a sound, and he drew himself up firmly to his full height.

"Then here's to Johnny Plank," he cried brazenly, hating the boys more than ever because they had seen him unbend. He broke into the villainous ditty:

Yo ho, yo ho, the frisky plank,
You walks along it so,
Till it goes down and you goes down
To Davy Jones below!

To terrorize the prisoners the more, though with a certain loss of dignity, he danced along an imaginary plank, grimacing at them as he sang; and when he finished he cried, "Do you want a touch of the cat before you walk the plank?"

At that they fell on their knees. "No, no," they cried so piteously that every pirate smiled.

"Fetch the cat, Jukes," said Hook; "it's in the cabin."

The cabin! Peter was in the cabin! The children gazed at each other.

"Ay, ay," said Jukes blithely, and he strode into the cabin. They followed him with their eyes; they scarce knew that Hook had resumed his song, his dogs joining in with him:

Yo ho, yo ho, the scratching cat,
Its tails are nine, you know,
And when they're writ upon your back—

What was the last line will never be known, for of a sudden the song was stayed by a dreadful screech from the cabin. It wailed through the ship, and died away. Then was heard a crowing sound which was well understood by the boys, but to the pirates was almost more eerie than the screech.

"What was that?" cried Hook.

"Two," said Slightly solemnly.

The Italian Cecco hesitated for a moment and then swung into the cabin. He tottered out, haggard.

"What's the matter with Bill Jukes, you dog?" hissed Hook, towering over him.

"The matter wi' him is he's dead, stabbed," replied Cecco in a hollow voice.

"Bill Jukes dead!" cried the startled pirates.

"The cabin's as black as a pit," Cecco said, almost gibbering, "but there is something terrible in there: the thing you heard crowing."

The exultation of the boys, the lowering looks of the pirates, both were seen by Hook.

"Cecco," he said in his most steely voice, "go back and fetch me out that doodle-doo."

Cecco, bravest of the brave, cowered before his captain, crying "No, no"; but Hook was purring to his claw.

"Did you say you would go, Cecco?" he said musingly.

Cecco went, first flinging up his arms despairingly. There was no more singing, all listened now; and again came a death-screech and again a crow.

No one spoke except Slightly. "Three," he said.

Hook rallied his dogs with a gesture. " 'Sdeath and odds fish," he thundered, "who is to bring me that doodle-doo?"

"Wait till Cecco comes out," growled Starkey, and the others took up the cry.

"I think I heard you volunteer, Starkey," said Hook, purring again.

"No, by thunder!" Starkey cried.

"My hook thinks you did," said Hook, crossing to him. "I wonder if it would not be advisable, Starkey, to humor the hook?"

"I'll swing before I go in there," replied Starkey doggedly, and again he had the support of the crew.

"Is it mutiny?" asked Hook more pleasantly than ever. "Starkey's ringleader."

"Captain, mercy," Starkey whimpered, all of a tremble now.

"Shake hands, Starkey," said Hook, proffering his claw.

Starkey looked round for help, but all deserted him. As he backed Hook advanced, and now the red spark was in his eye. With a despairing scream the pirate leapt upon Long Tom and precipitated himself into the sea.

"Four," said Slightly.

"And now," Hook asked courteously, "did any other gentleman say mutiny?" Seizing a lantern and raising his claw with a menacing gesture, "I'll bring out that doodle-doo myself," he said, and sped into the cabin.

"Five." How Slightly longed to say it. He wetted his lips to be ready, but Hook came staggering out, without his lantern.

"Something blew out the light," he said a little unsteadily.

"Something!" echoed Mullins.

"What of Cecco?" demanded Noodler.

"He's as dead as Jukes," said Hook shortly.

His reluctance to return to the cabin impressed them all unfavorably, and the mutinous sounds again broke forth. All pirates are superstitious; and Cookson cried, "They do say the surest sign a ship's accurst is when there's one on board more than can be accounted for."

"I've heard," muttered Mullins, "he always boards the pirate craft at last. Had he a tail, captain?"

"They say," said another, looking viciously at Hook, "that when he comes it's in the likeness of the wickedest man aboard."

"Had he a hook, captain?" asked Cookson insolently; and one after another took up the cry, "The ship's doomed." At this the children could not resist raising a cheer. Hook had well-nigh forgotten his prisoners, but as he swung round on them now his face lit up again.

"Lads," he cried to his crew, "here's a notion. Open the cabin door and drive them in. Let them fight the doodle-doo for their lives. If they kill him, we're so much the better; if he kills them, we're none the worse."

For the last time his dogs admired Hook, and devotedly they did his bidding. The boys, pretending to struggle, were pushed into the cabin and the door was closed on them.

"Now, listen," cried Hook, and all listened. But not one dared to face the door. Yes, one, Wendy, who all this time had been bound to the mast. It was for neither a scream nor a crow that she was watching; it was for the reappearance of Peter.

She had not long to wait. In the cabin he had found the thing for which he had gone in search: the key that would free the children of their manacles; and now they all stole forth, armed with such weapons as they could find. First signing to them to hide, Peter cut Wendy's bonds, and then nothing could have been easier than for them all to fly off together; but one thing barred the way, an oath, "Hook or me this time." So when he had freed Wendy, he whispered to her to conceal herself with the others, and himself took her place by the mast, her cloak around him so that he should pass for her. Then he took a great breath and crowed.

To the pirates it was a voice crying that all the boys lay slain in the cabin; and they were panic-stricken. Hook tried to hearten them; but like the dogs he had made them they showed him their fangs, and he knew that if he took his eyes off them now they would leap at him.

"Lads," he said, ready to cajole or strike as need be, but never quailing for an instant, "I've thought it out. There's a Jonah aboard."

"Ay," they snarled, "a man wi' a hook."

"No, lads, no, it's the girl. Never was luck on a pirate ship wi' a woman on board. We'll right the ship when she's gone."

Some of them remembered that this had been a saying of Flint's. "It's worth trying," they said doubtfully.

"Fling the girl overboard," cried Hook; and they made a rush at the figure in the cloak.

"There's none can save you now, missy," Mullins hissed jeeringly.

"There's one," replied the figure.

"Who's that?"

195

"Peter Pan the avenger!" came the terrible answer; and as he spoke Peter flung off his cloak. Then they all knew who 'twas that had been undoing them in the cabin, and twice Hook essayed to speak and twice he failed. In that frightful moment I think his fierce heart broke.

At last he cried, "Cleave him to the brisket," but without conviction.

"Down, boys, and at them," Peter's voice rang out; and in another moment the clash of arms was resounding through the ship. Had the pirates kept together it is certain that they would have won; but the onset came when they were all unstrung, and they ran hither and thither, striking wildly, each thinking himself the last survivor of the crew. Man to man they were the stronger; but they fought on the defensive only, which enabled the boys to hunt in pairs and choose their quarry. Some of the miscreants leapt into the sea; others hid in dark recesses, where they were found by Slightly, who did not fight, but ran about with a lantern which he flashed in their faces, so that they were half blinded and fell an easy prey to the reeking swords of the other boys. There was little sound to be heard but the clang of weapons, an occasional screech or splash, and Slightly monotonously counting—five—six—seven—eight—nine—ten—eleven.

I think all were gone when a group of savage boys surrounded Hook, who seemed to have a charmed life, as he kept them at bay in that circle of fire. They had done for his dogs, but this man alone seemed to be a match for them all. Again and again they closed upon him, and again and again he hewed a clear space. He had lifted up one boy with his hook, and was using him as a buckler, when another, who had just passed his sword through Mullins, sprang into the fray.

"Put up your swords, boys," cried the newcomer, "this man is mine."

Thus suddenly Hook found himself face to face with Peter. The others drew back and formed a ring round them.

For long the two enemies looked at one another; Hook shuddering slightly, and Peter with the strange smile upon his face.

"So, Pan," said Hook at last, "this is all your doing."

"Ay, James Hook," came the stern answer, "it is all my doing."

"Proud and insolent youth," said Hook, "prepare to meet thy doom."

"Dark and sinister man," Peter answered, "have at thee."

Without more words they fell to, and for a space there was no advantage to either blade. Peter was a superb swordsman, and parried with dazzling rapidity; ever and anon he followed up a feint with a lunge that got past his foe's defense, but his shorter reach stood him in ill stead, and he could not drive the steel home. Hook, scarcely his inferior in brilliancy, but not quite so nimble in wrist play, forced him back by the weight of his onset, hoping suddenly to end all with a favorite thrust, taught him long ago by Barbecue at Rio; but to his astonishment he found this thrust turned aside again and again. Then he sought to close and give the quietus with his iron hook, which all this time had been pawing the air; but Peter doubled under it and, lunging fiercely, pierced him in the ribs. At sight of his own blood, whose peculiar color, you remember, was offensive to him, the sword fell from Hook's hand, and he was at Peter's mercy.

"Now!" cried all the boys; but with a magnificent gesture Peter invited his opponent to pick up his sword. Hook did so instantly, but with a tragic feeling that Peter was showing good form.

Hitherto he had thought it was some fiend fighting him, but darker suspicions assailed him now.

"Pan, who and what art thou?" he cried huskily.

"I'm youth, I'm joy," Peter answered at a venture, "I'm a little bird that has broken out of the egg."

This, of course, was nonsense; but it was proof to the unhappy Hook that Peter did not know in the least who or what he was, which is the very pinnacle of good form.

"To 't again," he cried despairingly.

He fought now like a human flail, and every sweep of that terrible sword would have severed in twain any man or boy who obstructed it; but

Peter fluttered round him as if the very wind it made blew him out of the danger zone. And again and again he darted in and pricked.

Hook was fighting now without hope. That passionate breast no longer asked for life; but for one boon it craved: to see Peter show bad form before it was cold forever.

Abandoning the fight he rushed into the powder magazine and fired it.

"In two minutes," he cried; "the ship will be blown to pieces."

Now, now, he thought, true form will show.

But Peter issued from the powder magazine with the shell in his hands, and calmly flung it overboard.

What sort of form was Hook himself showing? Misguided man though he was, we may be glad, without sympathizing with him, that in the end he was true to the traditions of his race. The other boys were flying around him now, flouting, scornful; and as he staggered about the deck striking up at them impotently, his mind was no longer with them; it was slouching in the playing fields of long ago, or being sent up for good, or watching the wall-game from a famous wall. And his shoes were right, and his waistcoat was right, and his tie was right, and his socks were right.

James Hook, thou not wholly unheroic figure, farewell.

For we have come to his last moment.

Seeing Peter slowly advancing upon him through the air with dagger poised, he sprang upon the bulwarks to cast himself into the sea. He did not know that the crocodile was waiting for him; for we purposely stopped the clock that this knowledge might be spared him: a little mark of respect from us at the end.

He had one last triumph, which I think we need not grudge him. As he stood on the bulwark looking over his shoulder at Peter gliding through the air, he invited him with a gesture to use his foot. It made Peter kick instead of stab.

At last Hook had got the boon for which he craved.

"Bad form," he cried jeeringly, and went content to the crocodile.

Thus perished James Hook.

"Seventeen," Slightly sang out; but he was not quite correct in his figures. Fifteen paid the penalty for their crimes that night; but two reached the shore: Starkey to be captured by the redskins, who made him nurse for all their papooses, a melancholy come-down for a pirate; and Smee, who henceforth wandered about the world in his spectacles, making a precarious living by saying he was the only man that Jas. Hook had feared.

Wendy, of course, had stood by taking no part in the fight, though watching Peter with glistening eyes; but now that all was over she became prominent again. She praised them equally, and shuddered delightfully when Michael showed her the place where he had killed one; and then she took them into Hook's cabin and pointed to his watch which was hanging on a nail. It said "half-past one"!

The lateness of the hour was almost the biggest thing of all. She got them to bed in the pirates' bunks pretty quickly, you may be sure; all but Peter, who strutted up and down on deck, until at last he fell asleep by the side of Long Tom. He had one of his dreams that night, and cried in his sleep for a long time, and Wendy held him tight.

ROBERT LOUIS STEVENSON'S

A Child's Garden
of Verses

Time To Rise

A birdie with a yellow bill
Hopped upon the window sill,
Cocked his shining eye and said:
'Ain't you 'shamed, you sleepy-head?

The Cow

The friendly cow all red and white,
   I love with all my heart:
She gives me cream with all her might,
   To eat with apple-tart.

The Swing

How do you like to go up in a swing,
Up in the air so blue?
Oh, I do think it the pleasantest thing
Ever a child can do!

Up in the air and over the wall
Till I can see so wide,
Rivers and trees and cattle and all
Over the countryside—

Till I look down on the garden green,
Down on the roof so brown—
Up in the air I go flying again,
Up in the air and down!

A Good Play

We built a ship upon the stair
All made of the back-bedroom chairs,
And filled it full of sofa pillows
To go a-sailing on the billows.

We took a saw and several nails,
And water in the nursery pails;
And Tom said, "Let us also take
An apple and a slice of cake"—
Which was enough for Tom and me
To go a-sailing on, till tea.

We sailed along for days and days,
And had the very best of plays;
But Tom fell out and hurt his knee,
So there was no one left but me.

At the Sea-Side

When I was down beside the sea
A wooden spade they gave to me
To dig the sandy shore.

My holes were empty like a cup,
In every hole the sea came up,
Till it could come no more.

The Land of Story-Books

At evening when the lamp is lit,
Around the fire my parents sit;
They sit at home and talk and sing,
And do not play at anything.

Now, with my little gun I crawl
All in the dark along the wall,
And follow round the forest track
Away behind the sofa back.

There, in the night, where none can spy,
All in my hunter's camp I lie,
And play at books that I have read
Till it is time to go to bed.

These are the hills, these are the woods,
These are my starry solitudes;
And there the river by whose brink
The roaring lions come to drink.

I see the others far away.
As if in firelit camp they lay,
And I, like to an Indian scout,
Around their party prowled about.

So, when my nurse comes in for me,
Home I return across the sea,
And go to bed with backward looks
At my dear land of Story-Books.

207

My Shadow

I have a little shadow that goes in and out with me,
And what can be the use of him is more than I can see.
He is very, very like me from the heels up to the head;
And I see him jump before me, when I jump into my bed.

Happy Thought

The world is so full of a number of things,
I'm sure we should all be as happy as kings.

The Little Land

When at home alone I sit
And am very tired of it,
I have just to shut my eyes
To go sailing through the skies—
To go sailing far away
To the pleasant Land of Play;
To the fairy land afar
Where the Little People are;
Where the clover-tops are trees,
And the rain-pools are the seas,
And the leaves like little ships
Sail about on tiny trips;
And above the daisy tree
  Through the grasses,
High o'erhead the Bumble Bee
  Hums and passes.

The Wind

I saw you toss the kites on high
And blow the birds about the sky:
And all around I heard you pass,
Like ladies' skirts across the grass—
 O wind, a-blowing all day long,
 O wind, that sings so loud a song!

I saw the different things you did,
But always you yourself you hid.
I felt you push, I heard you call,
I could not see yourself at all—
 O wind, a-blowing all day long,
 O wind, that sings so loud a song!

A Child's Thought

At seven, when I go to bed,
I find such pictures in my head:
Castles with dragons prowling round,
Gardens where magic fruits are found;
Fair ladies prisoned in a tower,
Or lost in an enchanted bower;
While gallant horsemen ride by streams
That border all this land of dreams
I find, so clearly in my head
At seven, when I go to bed.

Foreign Lands

Up into the cherry-tree
Who should climb but little me?
I held the trunk with both my hands
And looked abroad on foreign lands.

I saw the next-door garden lie,
Adorned with flowers before my eye,
And many pleasant places more
That I had never seen before.

I saw the dimpling river pass
And be the sky's blue looking-glass;
The dusty roads go up and down
With people tramping in to town.

If I could find a higher tree
Farther and farther I should see,
To where the grown-up river slips
Into the sea among the ships,

To where the roads on either hand
Lead onward into fairy land,
Where all the children dine at five,
And all the playthings come alive.

—— ❧❧ ——

American Tales

Brer Rabbit and the Tar-Baby

R eal early one mornin', when Ol' Mister Sun was still gettin' his-self some shut-eye, Brer Fox went to work and got hisself some tar, and he mix it wid some turpentine, and fix up a contraption what he call a Tar-Baby. Den he took dis here Tar-Baby and he set her down smack in de middle of de road. And den he goes and hides hisself off in de bushes.

Now I don't have to tell you dat dis was de very same road Brer Rabbit went walkin' along every mornin', and 'fore long here comes Brer Rabbit pacin' down de road—lippity-clippity, clippity-lippity—jest as sassy as a jaybird. Brer Fox, he lay low.

Brer Rabbit, he prances along 'til he spies de Tar-Baby. Den he sets up on his hind legs like he wuz astonished. De Tar-Baby, she jest sets there, and Brer Fox, he lay low.

"Good Mawnin'!" says Brer Rabbit. "Nice wedder we havin' this mawnin'," says he.

De Tar-Baby don't say nothin', and Brer Fox, he lay low.

214

"Is you sick or somethin'? How your symptoms bin shapin' up now?" says Brer Rabbit.

De Tar-Baby don't say nothin', and Brer Fox, he wink his eye slow, and he lay low.

"Is you deaf?" says Brer Rabbit. "Cuz if you is, I can holler louder," says he, and den he starts hollerin' fit to raise the dead. "GOOD MAWNIN'! FINE, FINE WEDDER WE HAVIN' THIS MAWNIN', AIN'T IT?" says he.

De Tar-Baby don't say nothin', and Brer Fox, he lay low.

"You is stuck-up, dat's what you is," says Brer Rabbit. "And I'm goin' to cure you, dat's what I'm goin' to do," says he.

But de Tar-Baby jest stay still, and Brer Fox, he sort-a chuckle in his stomach.

"Yes sir. I'm goin' to learn you how to talk to respectable folks if it's de last thing I do," says Brer Rabbit. "If you don't take off dat hat and tell me good mawnin', I'm goin' to bust you wide open," says he.

De Tar-Baby don't say nothin', and Brer Fox, he lay low.

Brer Rabbit, he keep on askin' de Tar-Baby to say howdy, and de Tar-Baby, she jest keep on sayin' nothin'. Den presently, Brer Rabbit draws back wid his fist, and *blip*! He knock her in de side of de head. Right there's where he broke de molasses jug, cuz his fist, it gets stuck, and he can't pull loose. De tar held him there. But de Tar-Baby, she jest stay still, and Brer Fox, he lay low.

"If you don't lemme loose, I'll knock you again," says Brer Rabbit, and wid dat he go and swipe her wid de other hand, and dat stuck, too.

De Tar-Baby, she don't say nothin', and Brer-Fox, he lay low.

"Turn me lose, 'fore I kick de natural stuffin' out of you," says Brer Rabbit, and he's hollerin' now for sure.

But de Tar-Baby don't say nothin'. She jest hold on, and den Brer Rabbit kick wid one foot and den de other, and he lose de use of his feet in de same way. And Brer Fox, he lay low.

Den Brer Rabbit, he squall out dat if de Tar-Baby don't turn him a'loose he's goin' to butt her cranksided. And den he butted and his head is stuck, too.

Dat's when Brer Fox, come saunterin' forth, lookin' jest as innocent as one of your momma's mockin'birds.

"Howdy, Brer Rabbit," says Brer Fox. "You lookin' sort-a stuck-up dis mawnin'," says he. And den he roll on de ground, and laugh 'til he can't laugh no more. "I reckon you'll take dinner wid me, Brer Rabbit," says he. "I reckon you'll have to, cuz I ain't goin' to take no excuses."

Brer Rabbit, he don't say nothin'.

"I reckon I got you dis time," says Brer Fox. "Maybe I ain't, but I reckon I do," says he. "You been runnin' 'round here sassin' me for a mighty long time, but I reckon you done come to de end of de road. You been cuttin' up your capers and bouncin' 'round dis neighborhood 'til you come to believe yourself de boss of de whole gang. And you is always somewheres where you ain't got no bizness," says Brer Fox, says he. "Who ax you for to come and strike up an acquaintance wid dis here Tar-Baby? And who stuck you up there where you is? Nobody in de roun' world. You jest up and jammed yourself in on dat Tar-Baby widout waitin' for any invite," says Brer Fox. "And there you is and there you'll stay, cuz I reckon you know what—I mean *who*—I is havin' for my dinner tonight! Soon as I fixes up a brush-pile and fires her up, I'm goin' to bobbycue you dis very day, for sure," says Brer Fox, says he.

Den Brer Rabbit, he talk mighty humble.

"I don't care what you do wid me, Brer Fox," he says, "jest so you don't fling me in dat brier-patch. Roast me, Brer Fox," he says, "but jest please don't fling me in dat brier-patch!" says he.

"It's so much trouble fer to kindle a fire," says Brer Fox, "dat I reckon I'll have to hang you instead."

"Hang me jest as high as you please, Brer Fox," says Brer Rabbit, "but do don't fling me in dat brier-patch!" says he.

"I ain't got no rope," says Brer Fox, "so now I reckon I'll have to drown you."

"Drown me jest as deep as you please, Brer Fox," says Brer Rabbit, "but do don't fling me in dat brier-patch!" says he.

"Der ain't hardly no water in de creek," says Brer Fox, "so now I reckon I'll have to skin you instead."

"Skin me, Brer Fox," says Brer Rabbit. "Snatch out my eyeballs, tear out my ears by de roots, and cut off my legs," says he, "but do, *please*, Brer Fox, don't fling me in dat brier-patch," says he.

'Course Brer Fox, he wants to hurt Brer Rabbit jest as bad as he can, so he catch him by de back legs and sling him right in de middle of de brier-patch. There wuz a considerable commotion when Brer Rabbit struck de bushes, and Brer Fox sort-a hung around to see what wuz goin' to happen. By 'n' by, he hear somebody call him. Den, way up de hill, he sees Brer Rabbit settin' cross-legged on a chinkapin log combin' de pitch outta his hair with a chip. Den Brer Fox know dat he been tricked mighty bad. And Brer Rabbit he grin cuz he wuz pleased to fling back some of his sass. So he hollers out:

"Bawn and bred in a brier-patch, Brer Fox! Bawn and bred in a brier-patch!" And with dat he skip out jest as lively as a cricket in de embers!

Johnny Appleseed

Many years ago, when the United States was just a young country, there lived a man named Johnny Appleseed. He wasn't very tall, and he had a long scraggly beard, a great big grin, and eyes as blue as the bluest cornflowers. Now some folks said Johnny Appleseed was a strange-looking fellow because he wore a pair of patched pants and used an old piece of rope for a belt. Sometimes he wore a patched-up old shirt, and sometimes he wore no shirt at all! He didn't even own a pair of shoes! Instead of a hat, he wore an old mush-pot on his head. And over his shoulder he always carried a big old leather pouch stuffed full of appleseeds.

Johnny Appleseed wasn't always called that. As a small boy he was called John Chapman, or plain old Johnny for short.

He was born in what is now the state of Massachusetts. In those days, Massachusetts was a green land of rolling hills and well-tended farms. Best of all, as far as Johnny was concerned, there were plenty of apple orchards near his home. Johnny was sure that nothing in the world could

possibly taste as good as a ripe apple freshly picked off the tree. He liked everything made with apples, too—apple pie, apple cider, applesauce, and apple dumplings.

As he was growing up, he spent as much time as he could in apple orchards. He liked being there in spring when the trees were covered with white blossoms and even better in the fall when all the apples were ripe. It seemed to him that heaven must be like an apple orchard with apples enough for everyone.

When Johnny grew up, he got a job helping a farmer tend his apple orchard. Although Johnny wasn't very tall, he was strong and he worked hard, and the farmer was pleased with him. No one, the farmer liked to say, could possibly know more about apples than Johnny Chapman did. The farmer joked that Johnny should be called "Johnny Apple" or better yet, "Johnny Appleseed," and that was how Johnny got his name.

The American Revolution had recently ended, and the United States was an independent country now. People began to move into territories where no settlers had been before. There they planned to build cabins and start farms. Every day Johnny watched as families packed their belongings into covered wagons and began their journeys westward.

"I wonder where these folks will get apples out there," Johnny said to himself one day. He couldn't imagine not having any apples. Why, then there'd be no apple dumplings, no apple fritters, no apple pies, and no apple cider! It seemed like just about the worst thing Johnny could imagine. He worried about it and puzzled about it until one night he had a dream.

In the dream Johnny was wandering through a great apple orchard—bigger and more beautiful than any he had ever seen. Then an angel appeared. "Johnny," it called. "Johnny Appleseed! I want you to go on a journey for me. You must travel west across the great forests and prairies and mountains. Take with you a sack of apple seeds and plant them wherever you go. That way apple trees will grow everywhere, and there will be apples enough for everyone."

When Johnny woke up, the sun was shining. The sky was as blue as the bluest cornflower, and Johnny knew that he must do as the angel had told him. So he got a big leather pouch and filled it with different kinds of apple seeds. There were seeds for red Baldwin apples and tart Rhode Island Greenings, seeds for cooking apples and eating apples, for golden apples and russet apples, and for many other kinds of apple.

Then Johnny set out in the clothes he was wearing. Along the way it started to rain, and he realized he'd forgotten to put on a hat. The rain fell harder and harder. Then, just when it was at its hardest, Johnny spotted an old mush-pot lying by the side of the road. "That'll keep the rain off me!" Johnny thought. "And it'll make a fine pot to cook in, too!" And so he set it on his head and continued on his way. And that's how Johnny Appleseed got his mush-pot hat!

For many years Johnny roamed all over the land, planting apple seeds wherever he went. After a time, his boots got so worn out they fell off his feet! Since Johnny didn't want to stop to make a new pair, he just went on barefoot. He discovered, for some strange reason, he didn't really need any shoes. Even when the ground was white with snow, his feet never got cold. They never hurt him either, even when he walked on the rockiest roads. Some say this was because Johnny's angel was looking out for him.

Johnny never carried a knife or a gun either, but the wildest wild creatures never troubled him. Even fierce grizzly bears and mountain lions acted meek and mild around Johnny Appleseed, for he was a friend to all wild things.

One day, Johnny came upon a big old gray wolf caught in a trap. He felt sorry for the creature so he set it free and bandaged its wounded leg. After that, the old wolf followed Johnny wherever he went, running alongside him just like a tame dog. Settlers usually shot at wolves, but they knew to leave Johnny's pet alone. And so the old gray wolf became Johnny's closest companion.

Settlers were moving farther and farther west each year, and Johnny followed them. He planted apple seeds wherever people settled, so that there would be apples in all the new towns and villages and farms across America. Once a year or so, Johnny traveled back East to get more apple seeds. Along the way he always stopped to visit the pioneer families he had met on his earlier journeys. He liked to see the children growing up and the log cabins and farms the settlers had built. But best of all, he liked to look at all the apple trees he had planted. It always made him happy to see how tall and strong they had grown and to taste the apples they bore.

Years passed, and still Johnny traveled. His friend the gray wolf died, and so he went on alone. The pioneers he had first met were now old, and their children had grown up and taken over the farms. Johnny himself was old now, too. His red scraggly beard was as white as snow, and his face was as wrinkled as an old apple. But his smile was still as wide as ever, and his eyes were the same bright blue.

One cold winter day, Johnny got caught in a terrible storm. Snow and ice fell across the road, and even to Johnny it felt too cold to camp outside.

So he walked twenty miles to a log cabin that belonged to a settler he knew. When he got there, however, the cabin was empty. The family had gone to town to visit friends, and their front door was locked. Johnny spread his blanket on their front porch and stretched out for the night. Outside the moon shone brightly, and the world was covered with snow.

As Johnny closed his eyes, something strange happened. It seemed to him that it had suddenly grown as warm as a summer day, and all around him he could smell apples ripening. With a smile on his face, he drifted off to sleep and soon began to dream.

In his dream he was once again walking in a beautiful apple orchard with the same angel who had appeared before him so many years before. "Johnny," it called. "Johnny Appleseed! I've been looking for you. I've come to take you away with me." And it stretched out its hand toward him.

"But what about my apple trees?" Johnny cried. "I still have seeds that need planting."

The angel smiled at him and looked very bright and beautiful. "Johnny," it said, "you've done all I asked and more, and all your apple trees will grow strong and bear fruit for many generations. Now it is time for you to leave this world. But don't worry. Where I am taking you there is a garden, and in that garden there is a corner where you can plant your apple seeds."

"Very well," Johnny said, "then I'll come with you." So he took the angel's hand, and together they rose into the sky.

The next day the settler came home and found Johnny Appleseed lying on the porch as if he were sleeping. There was a smile on his face, and, it is said, in his hand was a ripe red apple!

Johnny's trees have grown tall and old. And every year, all across America, farmers pick apples that come from the trees Johnny Appleseed planted so long ago. In fact, the next apple you eat just might be one of them!

John Henry

The night John Henry was born, the moon was red and the sky was black. The wind howled and the rain poured. Lightning flashed and thunder rolled. Panthers growled and owls hooted and the Mississippi River ran a thousand miles upstream. Right on the stroke of midnight, John Henry was born—with a hammer in his hand!

His daddy looked at him and then looked out at the storm. "All this goin's-on has got to mean somethin'," he said. "And I reckon it's telling us that we ain't got no ordinary baby here. We got ourselves a *real* man!"

John Henry was awfully big and strong for a newborn baby. He grew fast, getting bigger and stronger every day. As he learned to crawl around the house his hammer rang out—*bang! bang!* Soon he was walking, and by the time he was four years old, John Henry was big enough to help with the chores.

"Honey," his mama said to him one day, "I know how you love that hammer. But your daddy needs your help picking cotton and hoeing corn. So you're gonna have to set your hammer down a while."

John Henry always did what his mama told him, so he hung his hammer up on the wall. Then he stared up at it, and he whispered, "Mama, I just know that hammer's gonna be the death of me one day."

John Henry worked beside his father. He weeded and he hoed. He pushed a plow across the fields. And he listened when his daddy told him, "If you do a job, son, you may as well do it right." Before long, John Henry had learned to use an axe, a saw, and a chisel. But nothing felt as good in his hands as a hammer.

At last, one evening when he was almost full-grown, John Henry went to his daddy and his mama and said, "You always told me how I was a real man, and real men should do what they do best. All this hoein' and plowin' ain't natural to me. I gotta find a job where I got a hammer in my hand."

His daddy nodded sadly and his mama cried a little. But they both knew John Henry was right. "Go on then, son," his daddy said. "You got to find your own way and your own star so you can be what you're meant to be."

So John Henry packed up his hammer and his other belongings and set off.

It wasn't long before he had a job as a cotton picker on a large plantation. He picked cotton from dawn to dusk under the blazing hot sun. No one had ever picked cotton like John Henry did—four thousand pounds a day! After a while, though, he decided he had to move on. The owner begged him to stay and offered to pay him more money, but John Henry only shook his head.

"Lord knows I don't mind hard work," he said, "but I'm a real man and this work ain't natural to me. I need the feel of a hammer in my hand!"

Down the road a ways, John Henry came to the edge of the great Mississippi River. There he saw a riverboat named the *Diamond Joe* pulling into port. John Henry stared at it and thought, "Maybe if I get me a job on that riverboat, it'll carry me far away—someplace where they got a need for a real man like me, a man with a hammer in his hand." So he went straight away and spoke to the captain.

The captain took one look at him and hired him on the spot. Any employer would, for years of hard labor had made John Henry so strong that his legs were as thick as tree trunks and his arms looked as if they were carved of iron. John Henry's job was to load the heavy cargo on board and to feed the furnace with great shovelfuls of wood and coal.

The *Diamond Joe* sailed up and down the great Mississippi River— past big lively cities and small pleasant towns, past wide green fields and cool dark forests. There were always new places to see, but none of them seemed to have a need for a man like John Henry.

One summer night, John Henry stood on deck and stared up at the sky. He remembered what his daddy had told him when they said good-bye, and he shook his head. "I ain't found it yet," he whispered. "I ain't found the road and the star for me!" He looked up at the sky and wondered which of all the stars was his.

Suddenly, the *Diamond Joe* gave a great lurch as the bottom of the boat scraped the riverbed and came to a sudden stop.

"We've run aground!" the first mate shouted.

"She's sinking fast!" the captain hollered. "If we don't get her off this sandbar, we're gonna capsize!"

"Captain," John Henry called, "maybe I can push the bow out of the mud!"

227

Then, before anyone on board could blink, he jumped off the boat into the muddy water. The mud came all the way up to his chest, but that didn't trouble John Henry. He just heaved and pushed as the captain shouted, "Full steam ahead!" Slowly, slowly the big riverboat began to move forward.

"Good God Almighty!" the pilot cried. "John Henry's pushin' us out of the mud!" Then John Henry gave one last might heave, setting the *Diamond Joe* afloat again. When John Henry climbed back aboard, the crew gathered around him, cheering and clapping him on the back.

Soon the *Diamond Joe* pulled into port for repairs, and John Henry decided to wander around town until the boat was ready. He found himself on a high bluff, and looking down, he saw a group of men laying a new railroad track. Some men took turns hammering big steel rods into the rock to break it up and make a level bed for the ties. Other men carried heavy steel rails and placed them across the wooden ties. Then others took huge steel hammers and pounded steel spikes into the ties. Sparks flew as steel struck steel, and the hammer strokes echoed through the air. The noise of those hammers sounded like church bells to John Henry.

"This is it!" he cried. "That's the work I was born to do, work fit for a real man with a hammer in his hand." He raced down the bluff and asked the track foreman to give him a job.

"You ever done any steel driving before?" the foreman asked, looking John Henry up and down.

John Henry drew himself up. "I was born with a hammer in my hand," he replied proudly. "This work's as natural to me as breathin' is."

Before the foreman could say no, John Henry reached down and took up a twelve-pound hammer. Then he joined two men who were driving steel rods into the rock. The first man struck the rod with a clang. The second one followed. John Henry raised his hammer high. It seemed like he'd been holding his breath all his life, waiting for this moment. Then

he brought his hammer
down with a mighty blow, right
on the head of that steel rod. With
just one blow John Henry sank that rod
all the way into the rock. The track foreman's
mouth fell open. The men standing around swore.
The sound of John Henry's mighty hammer stroke echoed
through the mountains.

"You're hired, friend!" the foreman shouted. "I ain't never seen a man who could drive steel like you can!"

So John Henry became a steel-driving man. Soon everybody up and down the railroad had heard about John Henry, for he was the best steel-driving man there ever was. Finally he had found the work he was made for.

Before long, John Henry found himself a wife, too. She was a slender, sweet-faced woman named Polly Ann, and he truly loved her. "I found my road and I found my star," he told himself. "And it don't seem like there's a thing left to wish for." Yet he still caught himself dreaming of doing something more, something extraordinary, though what that might be he couldn't say.

One day the head of the C & O railroad sent one of his men to offer John Henry a new job. He had heard all about John Henry and his hammer. The C & O was building a railroad track through the Big Bend Mountain in West Virginia. It would be the longest railroad tunnel ever made, and they wanted John Henry to do their steel-driving.

When John Henry saw the Big Bend Mountain, he could hardly believe his eyes. It was the biggest mountain he'd ever seen. He knew that the work would be difficult, but that didn't bother him. All he wanted was to hammer all day long and be the best steel-driving man in the world. So he took the job. The head of the company was glad. He knew the work would be hard and dangerous, but if John Henry led the way, the other men would follow.

Soon work on the Big Bend Tunnel began. First, John Henry and his men drilled deep holes in the mountainside. Then other men, called the powder boys, stuffed the holes with dynamite and blew out the rock. So the Big Bend Tunnel slowly began to take shape.

Deeper and deeper into the dark mountain the crew tunneled. But none of the men felt afraid, for they could always hear the sound of John Henry's hammer up ahead of them. It sounded like the beating of a strong, steady heart.

"Time to blast her out again," the crew boss said one day. The powder boys laid in the dynamite and lit the fuse. But as the fuse began burning down, the walls of the tunnel began to rumble and shake.

"It's a cave-in!" the men shrieked. John Henry and his crew scrambled for cover, but there was nowhere to go. They were trapped! Meanwhile, the fuse was still burning closer and closer to the dynamite.

"Hold on! I'll put her out!" John Henry hollered, and he raced to the fuse. He had almost reached it when he tripped and fell. There was no time to get up again. Whop! John Henry threw his mighty hammer! It landed right on the burning fuse a split hair before it reached the dynamite!

The flame sizzled out, and the men cautiously rose to their feet. They'd been saved by John Henry and his hammer.

"Ain't nothin' that John Henry can't do!" his men boasted. And a few days later John Henry proved it again. That day, the crew was hard at work when they heard a strange noise.

"What's that, boss?" asked John Henry's friend, Little Bill.

"I don't rightly know myself," replied John Henry.

Just then a big steel contraption came rumbling down the tunnel behind them, belching smoke and flames. "This here's a steam drill," the man from the railroad office told the foreman. "And it can do more work than any sixteen men combined!"

"I don't know about that," the foreman answered. "I got John Henry here and he's mighty good!"

"That's the truth all right," put in Little Bill, speaking up for his friend. "Ain't no machine in the world that can beat John Henry when his hammer's goin' strong!"

All the men cried, "John Henry can beat that thing!"

Then John Henry looked at the machine and said, "Yes sir, I reckon I could!"

So the railroad boss said they should have a contest the very next day—John Henry and Little Bill against the new steam drill.

The word quickly spread, and the next morning a thousand people gathered to see John Henry race against the new machine.

Polly Ann was up in front in her best blue dress. "Don't work yourself too hard, John Henry," she said.

"Don't worry," John Henry replied, kissing her for luck. "You watch, Polly, I'm gonna beat this thing!" With a pistol shot, the race began.

The machine screeched to life, and Little Bill positioned his drill. Then John Henry swung his mighty hammer, and as his hammer struck Bill's drill, the air all around sang.

Rattling and shaking, the machine blundered through the mountainside, and John Henry replied with stroke after mighty stroke. But it was no good. Through the sparks and smoke, Little Bill could see the steam drill was pulling ahead.

The race went on hour after hour, and still John Henry kept going as fast as ever. But the machine kept going, too.

Sweat poured down John Henry's face, and the handle of his hammer and Little Bill's drill grew red hot. So Polly Ann poured cool jugs of water over them to keep them going. And on they went, with the steam drill just ahead.

The sun began to sink in the sky. In the dark tunnel, John Henry turned to Little Bill and sang out:

"A man ain't nothin' but a man,
And before I let this machine beat me,
I'll die with a hammer in my hand.

That steam drill's still up ahead,
But I'll keep swingin' till I'm dead
And as this here hammer just won't do,

Go on, reach on down and hand me two,
Yeah, reach on down, Li'l Bill—
Yeah, reach on down and hand me two!"

So Little Bill handed him two twenty-pound hammers. And with one in either hand, John Henry started swinging. He swung those hammers so fast his arms became a blur. The rock crumbled and melted away before him. His great hammer strokes rang down the tunnel, and slowly John Henry and Little Bill began to pull even with the new steam drill! Finally the men and the machine were neck and neck. Suddenly, the machine started to cough and wheeze. Just as John Henry and Little Bill pulled ahead, the steam drill started chugging and shaking, then it choked and died.

John Henry had won the race! But even then, he didn't stop. He just kept right on going. A few minutes later, there was a great splintering sound, and slivers of rock flew all around. Bright, golden light came pouring into the black tunnel. John Henry had broken through to the other side of the mountain. The Big Bend Tunnel was finished.

John Henry stood there for a moment, staring at the last rays of the setting sun. Then as the crowd started cheering wildly, he turned and waved at his friends. Polly Ann rushed toward him, but before she could hug him, John Henry stumbled and fell to his knees.

"Get him a doctor," the track foreman shouted. But John Henry shook his head. Then he looked up at his Polly Ann. "I said that hammer was gonna be the death of me one day," he whispered. "Just make sure they write on my grave that I was a steel-drivin' man!" And taking his Polly Ann's hand, John Henry breathed his last.

The task had been too much for even his great heart, and so it was that John Henry died, still holding a hammer in his hand. Polly Ann had him buried right there at the mouth of the Big Bend Tunnel, and on his tombstone she had written just what he'd asked: "Here lies a steel-driving man!"

Although John Henry is gone, you can still hear him and his hammer singing all across this land. Whenever you hear a train rolling across the wide countryside or howling through a dark tunnel, listen! Whenever you hear train wheels squealing against those big steel rails, or a train whistle blowing at the midnight moon, listen! And you will hear the song of John Henry.

Paul Bunyan

Paul Bunyan was a lumberjack. He wore a red-and-black-checked shirt and a checked logging cap to match, and his blue jeans were held up with bright yellow suspenders. On his feet he wore heavy work boots, and in his hand he always carried an axe. There are more stories about Paul Bunyan than there are stars in the sky, but the one thing they all have in common is that they tell how Paul was the biggest and best lumberjack that ever lived.

When America was a young country, logging was an important business. The land was covered with dense forests of pine and spruce and mahogany and oak. It was a growing country, and the land had to be cleared to make way for farms and towns. Lumber was needed to build ships, houses, stores, and courthouses. That's where Paul Bunyan came in.

Most folks think Paul was born in Maine, close to the Canadian border. Although no one seems to agree exactly where Paul was born—or when—everyone does agree about one thing: He was a big baby.

It's said that at birth Paul weighed eighty-six pounds, give or take a few, and he grew bigger mighty quickly. Folks in Maine say that whenever Paul rolled over in his cradle, all his neighbors got worried. That's because just a little tossing and turning from Paul could knock down all the trees for miles around.

His poor mother hardly knew how to keep Paul fed. Why, in a single day her son would eat seventy-four buckets of oatmeal with five gallons of maple syrup poured on them and drink at least fourteen gallons of milk. Keeping him in clothes was an even bigger problem, for he grew so fast in all directions. At first, Paul's father made him a new pair of boots every day, but at last, he gave up. Paul would just have to go barefoot until his feet stopped growing!

One day Paul stopped growing. Everyone was relieved, because by that time Paul was as tall as the tallest pine tree. Now, that might be stretching the truth, but there's no question that Paul Bunyan was a mighty big fellow. You see, most folks came up only to Paul's ankles. Now that Paul was full-grown, he decided it was time for him to make his own way in the world. Paul's mother and father were sad to see him go, but secretly his mother couldn't help feeling a little relieved. As she told her husband, keeping that boy fed had become an impossible chore! So they climbed a great big ladder to kiss Paul good-bye. Then his father gave him a new pair of gigantic boots, and off Paul went.

Soon he came to a logging camp. Although Paul had no experience with logging, he talked the camp foreman into letting him try his hand. With one great cry of "Timber!" he swung his axe across twenty trees, bringing them all down with a single blow. The foreman's mouth dropped open, and he hired Paul on the spot!

Now, just about every other logger in the world would have been overjoyed to cut trees that fast, but not Paul! He wondered why he couldn't cut them down even faster. He puzzled over this until he came up with an answer.

The problem was his axe. Now, being as big as he was, Paul didn't use an ordinary axe. No, his axe had a head as big as a cow and a handle carved out of a whole pine tree. It worked pretty well at first, but when Paul really got it swinging, he had a bad habit of breaking the handle. He sure went through an awful lot of handles, until he decided to design himself a whole new axe.

First he got a fifty-yard piece of rope. Then he took the axe head off his old axe and tied it to the end of the rope. When the other loggers saw Paul's new axe, they just about died laughing. But their laughter didn't bother Paul. Gripping the rope tightly in his hands, Paul whirled the axe around him. The other loggers watched in amazement as Paul made forty trees fall to the ground with a single whirl of the rope!

Paul didn't stay at the logging camp long. If he had, there would have been no trees left for the other loggers to cut down, and they depended on the work so they and their families wouldn't starve. So Paul decided to strike out on his own. He traveled far and wide, harvesting lumber as he went for the nearest sawmill.

Then came the famous Winter of the Blue Snows. The weather was mighty unusual that year. Day after day, thick blue snow fell from the sky until the land, the rooftops, then the treetops were covered in blue. It got colder and colder, too, until nobody dared go outside—nobody, that is, except Paul Bunyan.

On one of those cold blue days, Paul took off into the woods, whistling to himself to stay warm. The trees sure looked beautiful with all that blue snow on them. Paul was busy looking around, when all of a sudden, he tripped over something, which he often did since his feet were so far below his eyes.

He looked down, and there, to his amazement, he saw a pair of great big hairy blue ears sticking out of the snow! Paul scratched his chin. Then he reached down and grabbed an ear in each hand. He pulled, and out of the snow popped a big blue baby ox.

The ox looked awfully cold, so Paul carried it back to his cabin. Once inside, he set the shivering ox down by the fire. All night long, Paul nursed the poor blue baby ox. When morning came, the young animal stood up, leaned over, and licked Paul on the cheek with her big, rough blue tongue. The licking tickled, and Paul burst out laughing. "Babe," he said, patting the ox's neck, "I got a feeling you and I are going to be great friends!" And that was how the blue ox got her name.

Paul was happier than he'd ever been. Now he had a partner to help him with his logging. He'd cut down the trees, and Babe, the Mighty Blue Ox, would haul them to the river where they floated to the sawmill. Like her master, Babe grew up to an enormous size. No one knows for sure how much Babe weighed, but it's said that the distance between her eyes measured exactly one hundred and forty axe handles, three jugs of maple syrup, and a plug of chewing tobacco all laid end to end!

Babe and Paul were wonderful friends, and Paul felt that, together, there was nothing they couldn't do. But, although Paul and Babe were the best logging team you could find, it was sometimes hard for them to find work. That's because no company could afford to keep the two of them fed!

Why, on just one average working day Paul Bunyan would have for dinner five bushels of fried potatoes, forty-five pounds of beefsteak, seven and a half hams, sixteen loaves of bread, thirteen dozen eggs, and to finish it all off, six hundred and seventy-eight pancakes topped with nine gallons of maple syrup. Paul would wash everything down with at least ten gallons of strong black coffee. So you can see why Paul and Babe weren't too popular with logging camp cooks.

So Paul decided to start a logging camp of his own. Paul's first logging camp was on the Onion River in the North Woods of Minnesota. He hired several hundred lumberjacks. Paul wanted this to be the biggest logging camp ever—and it was!

Old-time loggers who worked at Paul's camp claim it was so big that the men needed maps and compasses just to find their way around it. Some folks say he dug the Great Lakes to supply the camp with water. The cookhouse alone covered four square miles. Food was carried from the kitchen to the dining room by means of horse-drawn wagons, and there was a pipeline that brought warm maple syrup right to each table. I've heard on good authority that the food in Paul's camp was mighty good. Sourdough Sam, the camp cook, made a mean venison stew and some pure dee-lightful fried chicken. But Sam's sourdough pancakes were

every logger's all-time favorite. In fact, Sam was the world expert when it came to making pancakes, and sourdough pancakes were his own invention. They say Paul drained a small lake just so Sam would have enough room to mix his batter.

And the griddle was so big that the kitchen staff had to tie great slabs of bacon to their feet and skate across it just to keep it greased.

After a while, Paul grew a little restless. There were forests in parts of the United States that he'd never been to before. So he decided to make his logging camp into a traveling logging camp.

The very next day, Paul and his loggers set out westward across the United States. While traveling, they logged in the Dakotas, Oregon, Washington, and just about everywhere else. Now, all this tree-cutting might sound like it was unhealthy for the land, but Paul didn't do any harm. Although he cut many millions of trees, he was always careful to replace each one with a new seedling. He also always left a few trees standing in each forest. He did this because, as a boy, he'd learned that in order for the forest to flourish and grow, it must always be treated with respect.

Whenever a new job came up, Paul and his men would move the whole camp to it. This was easy. They'd simply place great big wheels under the dining room and the cookhouse and all the loggers' bunkhouses. Then Paul would link them all together with log chains and hook them to Babe's harness. Then the mighty blue ox would go to work, pulling the whole kit and caboodle behind her as if it were as light as a goose feather pillow.

One time Paul and his men were logging in Wisconsin. They had to use a road that was so crooked and tangled up that it couldn't even find its own way through the forest. The road was such a mess that loggers going back to camp on it would run right smack into themselves coming the other way! Paul knew something had to be done.

He considered the problem for a while, and then the solution came to him. He simply hitched Babe, the mighty blue ox, to the end of the road and called, "Come on, Babe! Pull! Pull!" Babe grunted and groaned and yanked as hard as she could. For a while nothing happened. Then, with a CRACK so loud it sounded as if the Earth were splitting in two, that crooked road lost all of its kinks and became as straight as the straightest ruler!

Paul loved solving tricky problems like that. In fact, problem solving was one of his favorite activities. Of course, one thing leads to another, and all this problem solving eventually led to some inventions. Paul invented the chain saw and the double-headed axe and just about all the other tools loggers use today.

And that's just the tip of the iceberg when it comes to Paul's many accomplishments. It was Paul who got the Round River to run straight and who dug the Saint Lawrence River. And when the Yellowstone River got frozen to the Missouri River during the Winter of the Big Snows, who do you think got them unstuck again?

Paul also created the Rocky Mountains and the Appalachian Mountains. Here's how he did it. See, when logging was at its height, some important people hired Paul and his crew to dig a canal across the middle of the country so logs could float back and forth. So Paul started digging. Whistling as he worked, he shoveled so fast that before long he built up a great big heap of dirt to the right and another one to the left. And that's how the Rockies came to be on one side of the United States and the Appalachians on the other.

When Paul was finished digging the canal, Babe kicked over a bucket of water and turned Paul's canal into the great Mississippi River. So you see, there wasn't much about the great outdoors that Paul wasn't mixed up in one way or another!

Now you're probably wondering whatever happened to Paul Bunyan, the greatest lumberjack of them all. Well, there's plenty of stories about that, too. But most folks claim that the United States was just getting too civilized for Paul and Babe so they headed north to Alaska—the only state truly big enough for the two of them.

Others, mostly loggers, insist that Paul Bunyan is still around the lower forty-eight. According to them, Paul's fame has made him a little retiring of late, and nowadays he spends all his time deep in the northern woods.

So, remember, if you're ever out walking in the woods one day and you hear a voice holler, "Timber!"—so loud it makes the whole forest shake—don't be too startled if you turn and find yourself looking right at the boot of Paul Bunyan, the greatest lumberjack of them all!

The Night Before Christmas

The Night
Before Christmas

Twas the night before Christmas,
 when all through the house
Not a creature was stirring,
 not even a mouse.

The stockings were hung by the chimney with care,
 In hopes that St. Nicholas soon would be there.
The children were nestled all snug in their beds,
 While visions of sugarplums danced in their heads;

More rapid than eagles his coursers they came,
And he whistled and shouted and called them by name:
"Now, Dasher! now, Dancer! now, Prancer and Vixen!
On, Comet! on, Cupid! on, Donder and Blitzen!
To the top of the porch! to the top of the wall!
Now dash away! dash away! dash away, all!"
As dry leaves that before the wild hurricane fly,
When they meet with an obstacle, mount to the sky,
So up to the housetop the coursers they flew,
With a sleigh full of toys—and St. Nicholas too.

And then, in a twinkling, I heard on the roof
The prancing and pawing of each little hoof.
As I drew in my head and was turning around,
Down the chimney St. Nicholas came with a bound.
He was dressed all in fur, from his head to his foot,
And his clothes were all tarnished with ashes and soot;

And Mama in her kerchief, and I in my cap,
   Had just settled our brains for a long winter's nap,
When out on the lawn there arose such a clatter,
   I sprang from my bed to see what was the matter.
Away to the window I flew like a flash,
   Tore open the shutters and threw up the sash.
The moon on the breast of the new-fallen snow
   Gave a lustre of midday to objects below;
When what to my wondering eyes should appear
   But a miniature sleigh and eight tiny reindeer,
With a little old driver, so lively and quick,
   I knew in a moment it must be St. Nick!

A bundle of toys he had flung on his back,
And he looked like a peddler just opening his pack.
His eyes, how they twinkled! his dimples, how merry!
His cheeks were like roses, his nose like a cherry!
His droll little mouth was drawn up like a bow,
And the beard on his chin was as white as the snow.
The stump of a pipe he held tight in his teeth,
And the smoke, it encircled his head like a wreath.
He had a broad face and a little round belly
That shook, when he laughed, like a bowl full of jelly.

He was chubby and plump, a right jolly old elf,
And I laughed when I saw him, in spite of myself.
A wink of his eye and a twist of his head
Soon gave me to know I had nothing to dread.

He spoke not a word, but went straight to his work,
   And filled all the stockings, then turned with a jerk,
And laying a finger aside of his nose,
   And giving a nod, up the chimney he rose.

He sprang to his sleigh, to his team gave a whistle,
    And away they all flew like the down of a thistle.
But I heard him exclaim, ere he drove out of sight,
    "Happy Christmas to all, and to all a good night!"

Hans Christian Andersen
Fairy Tales

The Ugly Duckling

It was a lovely summer day. The wheat was golden and wildflowers dotted the meadows. Beside them were cool forests with deep lakes. Near a green hedge by the water, a duck sat on her nest, waiting for her eggs to hatch. She had been sitting a long time and was getting tired. At last, one shell cracked, and then another. And from each egg a little duckling poked its head out and cried, "Cheep, cheep!"

The mother duck was overjoyed. "Quack! Quack!" she said happily. Then she saw that one egg had still not hatched. With a sigh, she settled back down on her nest.

"How are you getting on?" called an old duck who had come to pay her a visit.

"One of my eggs still hasn't hatched," replied the mother duck. "But look at all the others. Aren't they the prettiest ducklings you ever saw?"

"Indeed," the old duck agreed. "But let me look at the egg that won't hatch. It might be a turkey egg. Once I was tricked into hatching one, and after all my trouble, the young turkey wouldn't go in the water!"

The old duck peered at the egg, which was larger than the others and gray in color. "Yes," she said, "that's a turkey egg, all right. Just leave it alone, and come teach your own children how to swim."

But the mother duck refused. "I've been sitting here so long already," she said, "a few more days won't make any difference."

"Suit yourself," quacked the old duck, and waddled off.

The mother waited and waited. Then, with a crack the egg finally hatched, and out popped the last duckling. He was a very strange-looking duckling indeed! So large and gray! Even his mother had to admit that he was rather ugly.

"Oh dear," she thought. "Maybe it was a turkey egg, after all! However, I'll soon find out when we go in the water."

Early the next morning the mother duck led her brood to the river. It was a bright, sunny day, perfect for swimming. "Quack, quack," she cried, and jumped into the water with a big splash. One by one the ducklings followed her. At first, they sank to the bottom, but soon they all bobbed up again. And before long they all were swimming very nicely, including the ugly duckling.

"How skillfully he uses his feet," his mother said. "And how well he holds up his head! He's not a turkey. He is my very own duckling, after all! And, if you look at him closely, he is not really as ugly as all that!" Feeling very proud, she beckoned her ducklings out of the water and marched them toward the barnyard, for she wanted to introduce them to the other animals.

Along the way, she instructed her ducklings how to behave properly. "Hold up your head and don't turn in your toes," she said. "And bow to everyone, especially the old duck with the red rag tied around her leg. She is of Spanish blood and is very noble. Here we are. Now be sure to say 'quack' to everyone!"

The little ducklings had learned their lessons well and did as they were told. The older ducks looked them over carefully. "Another brood of

ducklings," sighed one large gray duck, "as if there weren't enough of us already!" Then he pointed to the ugly duckling. "This one is so big and awkward looking!" he said. "We don't want him here!" The large gray duck then bit the ugly duckling in the neck.

"He is not doing any harm!" the mother cried. "Leave him alone!"

The old duck with the red rag on her leg then spoke. "The others are very pretty," she said. "But that last duckling is very ugly!"

"That can't be helped," replied the mother. "But he swims very well and is polite and well-behaved. I'm sure he'll turn out all right."

"Very well," sighed the old duck. "He can stay. Make yourselves at home."

The other ducklings were treated well, and in a short time they felt comfortable in their new surroundings. But everyone was mean to the ugly duckling. Some ducks bit him. Some made fun of him. The chickens and geese teased him and bullied him. And the turkey cock, who acted as if he were king of the barnyard, said, "That duckling is so ugly I can't bear to look at him." Then he flew at the duckling and scratched him with his claws.

The ugly duckling's brothers and sisters were not kind to him either. "Oh, you ugly creature," they scoffed whenever they saw him. "How we wish the cat would get you!" Day by day, the animals' scorn grew worse. Finally one evening the ugly duckling overheard his mother say that she wished he would just disappear.

The ugly duckling was utterly miserable. He decided to run away. And so he flew over the hedge, frightening all the little birds who lived there.

"They are afraid of me because I am so ugly," the duckling thought. Then he flapped his wings and flew a ways to the great marsh where the wild ducks lived. There he settled for the night.

Early the next morning the wild ducks noticed the ugly duckling and stared at him with curiosity. "What kind of duck are you?" they asked. The ugly duckling bowed politely. "I don't know myself," he replied humbly. "Well," the wild ducks said. "You are certainly very ugly, but you seem nice enough. And so long as you don't wish to marry into our family, you may stay with us."

The ugly duckling agreed, and they all flew across the marsh together. But suddenly there was a loud POP! and two wild ducks fell dead among the reeds. Soon there were popping sounds all around. Hunters had surrounded the marsh and were firing at the wild ducks!

The ugly duckling was terrified. He hid in a clump of reeds, and soon a ferocious-looking hunting dog came running at him. It glared at the ugly duckling and sniffed him but didn't stop.

"I am so ugly that even a dog will not bite me," the ugly duckling thought. Then he lay very still until hours later the shots had stopped and the marsh was again quiet. He could still see where the wild ducks had fallen, and trembling all over, he flew toward the forest.

It was evening and a storm was rising. The rain began to fall so hard that the duckling could not go on. He stopped at a little cottage, and finding the door open, he walked inside.

An old woman lived in the cottage with her prize hen and a big tom-cat, which she loved very much. When the duckling entered, the hen began to cluck and the cat began to mew. The old woman, who was quite nearsighted, peered around the room and called out, "What's all that noise?" When she spotted the ugly duckling she was delighted. She thought that he was a nice, fat duck from a nearby farm. "What good luck," she cried. "I only hope you're not a drake, for I should dearly love to have some delicious duck's eggs!" Then she gave the ugly duckling some bread.

The hen and the cat scowled. They liked to think they were mistress and master of the household and were not at all pleased about their new guest.

"Can you lay eggs?" the hen asked the ugly duckling.

"No," he replied.

"Then what good are you?"

"Can you arch your back and purr?" the cat said.

"No," said the ugly duckling, hanging his head.

"Then what can you do?" demanded the cat.

"I can swim," replied the ugly duckling. And he told them how pleasant it was to swim in the cool water and then dive to the bottom.

"Pleasant!" cried the hen. "It sounds dreadful to me! Why, the cat is the cleverest creature I know, and he's told me many times how awful it is to get wet. If I were you, I'd forget about swimming and learn to lay eggs and purr, or you won't last here much longer!"

After that the hen pecked the ugly duckling and the cat scratched him whenever he got too close. At last, the duckling decided that he had better move on again.

He flew across the fields until he came to a big pond in the middle of the forest. Here he could swim and dive as much as he liked. But he was careful to avoid all other creatures, for he had grown so ashamed of his ugly appearance.

Autumn came, and the leaves on the trees turned red and gold. The wind grew sharper and colder, and all the leaves danced and whirled from the trees. Winter was coming. Soon the clouds grew thick and pale, and snow and hail fell. It was a difficult and lonely time for the ugly duckling.

One evening as the sun was setting, he sat at the edge of the pond, shivering and looking up at the sky. The clouds were radiant and bright. Flying overhead was a flock of the most beautiful birds he had ever seen. They were snow-white, with strong wings and long, graceful necks. The ugly duckling had never seen birds like these before. He did not know that they were swans flying south for the winter. Their feathers gleamed in the last rays of the sun. Spreading their wings, they uttered a cry unlike any he had heard, and they rose higher into the sky.

The ugly duckling marveled at the beautiful birds. Without knowing why, he stretched out his neck and called after them—a cry so strange it frightened him. And then the gorgeous birds were gone.

Although he did not know what they were called, he had never felt so close to any living creatures before. He felt a deep longing to be as proud and lovely as they were. "But what would such beautiful birds say if they were to see me?" the duckling thought.

The winter grew cold and fierce. Now the poor ugly duckling had to swim in circles all day long to keep the water from freezing over. Every night, the space he swam in grew smaller and smaller. At last, the pond froze so hard that the ice crackled. The ugly duckling became so exhausted from trying to keep a pool clear for swimming that he fainted and froze fast in the ice.

The next morning, a peasant who was passing by spotted the stiff, cold creature. He picked up the duckling and carried him home to his wife and children. The wife placed the ugly duckling near the warm fire, and soon he woke up. Wanting to play with the duckling, the children ran toward him. The quick movements, however, frightened the duckling so badly he fluttered up, knocking over the milk jug. Then he flew into the butter cask and the corn barrel and when he came out, what a sight he was! The woman screamed, running after him with a poker. The children laughed and tumbled over each other, trying to catch him. The poor ugly duckling barely managed to escape out the window! Exhausted and heartsick, he hid in the bushes.

It would be very sad to tell you all the hardships the ugly duckling endured during that long icy winter. But one day, he woke up to feel the warm sun shining on his back. Tiny green leaves had sprouted on the trees. Birds were singing, and flowers were poking out of the dark earth. It was spring, beautiful spring!

The ugly duckling flapped his wings. They felt so much stronger than before. He rose high in the air and flew until he came to a large garden. Apple trees blossomed there, and willow trees lined a clear stream, dipping their long branches into the cool water. It was such a beautiful and inviting spot! The ugly duckling flew down and settled beside the stream.

Soon three beautiful white swans came gliding toward him from across the water. Seeing the lovely birds made the ugly duckling feel sadder than ever. "If I, the ugly one, swim over to those royal birds," he said to himself, "they surely will kill me for daring to come near them. But I don't mind. Better to be killed by such lovely creatures than endlessly pecked by ducks and hens who hate me!"

Entering the stream, he slowly swam toward the proud swans. The moment they saw him, they rushed toward him, their wings raised high.

"Go ahead, kill me," whispered the ugly duckling, and he bent his head toward the water and waited to die.

He saw his reflection in the clear water. To his amazement, he was no longer a dark gray bird, awkward and ugly. Instead, his neck had grown long and graceful, and his feathers were as white as snow. To be born in a duck's nest in a barnyard makes no difference to a bird hatched from a swan's egg. The ugly duckling had grown into a beautiful swan!

The other three swans swam up to him and stroked his neck with their beaks in welcome. Soon some children came running into the garden and threw cake and bread crumbs into the water.

"Look," they cried. "There's a new swan. Why, he's the most beautiful one of all!"

When the once-ugly duckling heard that, he felt quite shy and hid his head under his wing. He had been teased and mistreated because of his ugliness, and now he heard himself being called the most beautiful of all birds. Looking around at the bright sunlight, the fresh, green trees, and the clear, sparkling water, he ruffled his feathers and cried, "I never dreamed I would ever be so happy when I was the ugly duckling!"

The Nightingale

❦❦❦

In China there once lived an emperor in the most beautiful palace in the world. It was built entirely of the finest porcelain and was so delicate and costly that it could be touched only with great care. Around the palace were the most splendid gardens full of rare flowers. The prettiest ones had silver bells tied to them so that they tinkled whenever anyone passed. The gardens were so large the gardener himself could not say where they ended. But those who traveled knew that at the edge of the gardens, there was a cool forest that sloped down to the deep blue sea.

And in this forest there lived a nightingale. The nightingale sang so beautifully that the poor fishermen, who worked hard casting their nets every minute of the day, stopped to listen. Hearing the nightingale's song somehow made their hearts lighter.

People from all over the world came to see the emperor's city with its beautiful porcelain palace and magnificent gardens. But on hearing the nightingale, they said, "This is the best of all." When they returned home, they spoke of what they had seen. Some even wrote books celebrating the beauty of the palace and the gardens. But their highest praise went to the nightingale. These books were read by people who lived all over the world, and one day the emperor was given one.

He read of the beauty of his city and of his exquisite porcelain palace and remarkable gardens, and he smiled and nodded. Then he read, "Yet of all these things, the nightingale is the most beautiful of all."

"What?" the emperor cried. "I have never heard of this nightingale! Is there such a bird in my kingdom? Why was I not told of it before?" But none of the emperor's lords, ladies, or courtiers had heard of the nightingale either.

"I must have the nightingale appear before me this very evening!" said the emperor. And he sent his most trusted courtier to find the nightingale and bid her to come to the palace at once.

The courtier searched the palace. He looked down every hall and passageway, up stairs and down stairs, until he was quite out of breath. He asked everyone he met about the nightingale. But no one knew anything about the bird.

At last the courtier came upon a kitchen maid who said, "The nightingale! Oh, yes. I know her well. Every evening I visit my poor sick mother, who lives by the deep blue sea. I am always tired when I start out. But as I pass through the dark forest, I hear the nightingale sing. I stop to listen. Her song always brings tears to my eyes, for I feel just as if my mother were kissing me."

"Ah," the courtier said, "if you will only lead me to this nightingale I promise that you will always have a place in the emperor's palace." The maid agreed. So she led the courtier and several ladies-in-waiting to the forest to find the nightingale.

They had not gone far when a cow began lowing.

"Oh," the courtier cried, "that must be the nightingale now. I know I have heard her song before. What power she has for such a small creature!"

The kitchen maid laughed. "That is not the nightingale," she replied. "That is only a cow. We have a long way to go yet."

Then they passed some frogs croaking in the marsh.

"How lovely," cried the courtier. "Why, her song sounds almost like church bells!"

"No," said the kitchen maid. "Those are only frogs, but we don't have long to wait now."

Just then the nightingale began to sing. "Listen!" the kitchen maid whispered, pointing to a small gray bird perched on a branch. "There she is!"

"Indeed," the ladies-in-waiting all cried, "she's a plain little thing, isn't she? We never imagined she would look like that!"

"Oh, nightingale," the kitchen maid called, "our great emperor wishes you to sing for him."

"With pleasure," the nightingale said. And she began to sing the loveliest song imaginable.

"It sounds like tiny bells of glass!" the courtier exclaimed. "Most unusual. I'm sure the nightingale will be a great success!"

"Shall I sing for the emperor again?" asked the nightingale, mistaking the courtier for His Majesty. "Oh no," the courtier said. Then he explained that the emperor wished her to present herself at court.

"My song sounds better in the green forest," the nightingale replied. "But I will gladly come."

In celebration that evening, the porcelain palace was lit with thousands of tiny silver and gold lanterns. All were dressed in their finest silks and satins. And placed beside the emperor's great golden throne was a golden perch for the nightingale. At last the nightingale was comfortably settled on her perch. The emperor then nodded at her to begin.

Her song was so lovely that tears came to the emperor's eyes and rolled down his cheeks. On and on the nightingale sang. The music grew more beautiful until it had touched the hearts of all who heard it. When the nightingale finished, the emperor was so delighted he said that he would give her his gold slipper to wear around her neck. But she refused it, saying, "I have seen tears in the eyes of the emperor, and that is reward enough."

The emperor was so delighted with the nightingale he commanded her to remain at the palace. She was given a golden cage and twelve servants to care for her. Everyone loved and admired the small bird. Some young ladies tried to mimic the bird, but to no avail.

About a month later, the emperor received a large package with the word *Nightingale* written on it. "Why, this must be another book about our wonderful bird," said the emperor. But inside he found instead an artificial nightingale. It was made of gold and adorned with precious jewels. Around its neck was a gold ribbon that said, "The Emperor of Japan's nightingale is nothing compared to that of the Emperor of China." When the gold bird was wound up, it sang like the real nightingale and even moved its tail up and down in time to the music.

When the courtiers saw the gold nightingale, they were very excited. "How beautiful it is!" they cried, and they insisted that the two nightingales sing together.

But the two did not sing well together, for the gold bird could sing only the same waltz over and over again, while the real nightingale sang her notes in her own natural way. Then the artificial nightingale was wound up and made to sing alone. Its singing was so perfectly regular. And it was certainly much prettier to look at than the real nightingale! Thirty times the courtiers listened to the gold nightingale sing its song. And if the emperor hadn't stopped them, they gladly would have listened to it a dozen times more! The emperor explained that the real nightingale must also be allowed to sing.

But when the courtiers went to summon the nightingale, they found that she was gone. She had flown out the window back to her home in the forest. "What an ungrateful bird!" they cried. And so the emperor

banished the nightingale from his kingdom. The artificial nightingale took her place in the golden cage beside the emperor's bed and was given his gold slipper to wear around its neck.

A year passed. Every night the court gathered to hear the gold nightingale sing. By this time, they knew every note of its song by heart, and that made them enjoy listening to it even more. One evening as the artificial nightingale sang for the emperor in his bed, there was a strange snapping sound. All the gears inside the bird started whirring, and the music came to a stop. The best doctors in the kingdom were called, but they could not fix the bird. At last, the emperor sent for the imperial watchmaker. He examined the artificial nightingale carefully and finally got it working again. However, he said that the mechanism was quite worn out and must be treated with care. This caused great sorrow at court, for now the gold nightingale could be wound up to sing only once a year.

Five years passed in this way, and then a great grief came upon the kingdom. The emperor became ill and was not expected to live much longer. The people were saddened, for they truly loved their emperor, but there was nothing they could do to help him.

They were sure that the old emperor would not live through the week. And so a new emperor was chosen to replace him.

In his room the emperor lay cold and pale on his golden bed. The silvery moon shone on him through the open window, and beside him, the gold nightingale sat silent in its golden cage. The emperor felt a strange weight on his chest, and he could scarcely breathe. When he opened his eyes, he saw Death staring at him. All around him he seemed to hear the murmuring of many voices, and when he peered into the shadows he saw all kinds of unfamiliar faces. Some of them were ugly; some were very beautiful. These were the emperor's good and bad deeds staring him in the face.

"Remember," they seemed to whisper. "Remember." The emperor felt himself growing colder. He longed suddenly to hear music, music that would drown out all the strange voices. He turned to the gold nightingale sitting in its cage. "Please sing," he begged it. "I have given you a cage of gold and my own gold slipper to wear around your neck. Please sing to me." But of course there was no one to wind the mechanical bird, so it remained silent.

Death stared with great, hollow eyes at the emperor. The room was terribly still. Suddenly, a burst of music came through the open window. The real nightingale was perched on a branch outside. She had heard about the emperor's illness and had come to sing for him.

She sang of summer days when the trees are green and fragrant and flowers bloom all around. She sang of golden mornings and quiet eve-

nings when the shadows in the forest are blue and still. As she sang the emperor felt the weight on his chest lighten and the blood stir in his veins. Even cold Death could not keep from listening to her song and begged her to go on, saying, "Sing, little nightingale, sing!"

So she sang of quiet gardens where roses bloom and the grass is covered by the dew of tears. Her song was so lovely it made Death himself grow weary and long to rest in the quiet of his own garden. At last, with a sigh, Death slipped out the window in a cloud of cold, gray mist.

"Thank you, thank you, nightingale!" the emperor cried. "I banished you from my kingdom once. Yet you came and sang to me and saved my life with your song. How can I ever repay you?"

"You have already rewarded me," said the nightingale, "when I saw tears in your eyes the first time I sang for you."

"You must stay with me always now," the emperor then said. "I will break the gold nightingale into a thousand pieces. I will give you a new golden cage and my gold slipper, and you shall sing only when it pleases you."

"No," the nightingale replied. "The gold bird did all it could. Keep it here with you. I cannot be happy living in a palace. But do not worry. I will come each evening and sing outside your window. I will sing of happy things and sad things, too. In my song, you will hear of great lords and poor fishermen, proud young ladies and tired old washerwomen, all the good and the evil of your kingdom, and my song will refresh you and make you think, too. I only ask that you keep my visits a secret and never let anyone know that you have a little bird who tells you everything."

Then the nightingale sang to the emperor again, and he fell into a deep, refreshing sleep. When he awoke the sun was shining and he felt strong and well.

His servants came to his door to look in at their dead emperor. Imagine how surprised they were when they saw him walk toward them and say, "Good morning!"

The Steadfast
Tin Soldier

O nce upon a time there were twenty-five tin soldiers. They were
brothers and had been made from the same large tin spoon.
They all stood very straight in their elegant red-and-blue
uniforms, shouldering their little tin guns. The first thing they ever heard
was a boy shouting, "Tin soldiers!" as he lifted the lid off the box where
they were lying. He had received them as a birthday present.

The boy set the tin soldiers out on the table. They were all exactly
alike, except for one, which had only one leg, for he was made last and
there had not been enough tin to finish him properly. Nevertheless, he
stood as straight as all the others.

The table where the tin soldiers stood was covered with toys. There
were brightly colored tops, china dolls, and a stuffed bear. But best of all,
there was a paper castle. It was so wonderfully constructed that little
rooms could be seen through its tiny windows. In front of it, a number of
painted paper trees stood around a small mirror, which was meant to rep-
resent a lake. Small wax swans swimming on the lake were reflected in

it. But most beautiful of all was the tiny paper dancer who stood in the door of the castle.

Her dress had a skirt of white tulle, and a blue silk ribbon encircled her little shoulders like a shawl. This ribbon was fastened with a bright silver sequin the size of her face. Her arms were stretched out before her, and one leg was lifted so high that the little tin soldier could not see it. "She must have only one leg like me," he thought. "She's the wife for me!" Then he sighed. "But she lives in a castle, while I have only a box, which I must share with all my brothers. That would never do for her. Still, I must get to know her!" So he stretched himself flat on the table behind a snuffbox so he could see her better. He watched as she stood very still. And even though her leg was raised high in the air, she didn't once lose her balance.

When evening came the children of the house put away the other tin soldiers and went to bed. That was when all the toys had their fun. They amused one another by giving balls, fighting battles, and paying visits. The tin soldiers rattled in their box, for they wanted to join in. The stuffed bear did somersaults and the nutcrackers played leapfrog. Even the pencil got up and danced a jig. Only the tin soldier and the dancer remained steadfast in their places.

The clock struck twelve, and a strange thing happened. The lid of the snuffbox sprang open. But instead of snuff inside, there was a little goblin who poked out his head and stared right at the tin soldier.

"Keep your eyes to yourself," the goblin said.

But the tin soldier pretended not to hear.

"Just you wait until tomorrow," the goblin said in a terrible voice, and he retreated into the snuffbox.

The next morning, the children picked up the little tin soldier and set him on the windowsill. I cannot say whether it was the goblin's doing or not, but, all of a sudden, a draft came up and knocked the tin soldier out the window. Down he fell three stories into the street below. It was terrible! He landed with his little tin gun stuck between two cobblestones and his one leg pointing up in the air. The little boy and one of the maids ran outside to look for him. They both stepped right next to him, but neither could find him. If he'd only shouted "Help, help!" they would have spotted him. But he was too proud to do that when he was in uniform!

It began to rain hard, and soon there was quite a downpour. When it ended, two boys came running up the street. "Look," one of them cried. "There's a tin soldier. Let's make him a boat to sail in."

So they made a boat out of an old sheet of newspaper and put the tin soldier in it. Then they sent him sailing down the gutter, while they ran alongside, clapping their hands. Such large waves rolled in the gutter, and how quickly the water flowed! The little paper boat rocked from side to side and bobbed up and down. Sometimes it spun around so quickly that the little tin soldier felt dizzy.

Yet he stood up straight and bravely shouldered his little gun, for he was a true soldier. Suddenly, the boat was pulled into a large drain and went whirling down a tunnel that was even darker than the tin soldier's box.

"What now?" he thought. "I am sure this is all that goblin's doing. Oh, if only the little dancer were here with me. Then I would not care if it were twice as dark!"

Just then a water rat, which lived in the drain, came chasing him. "Have you got a passport?" it squeaked, gnashing its teeth horribly. "Give it to me at once!"

But the tin soldier only stared straight ahead and clung to his little gun. The rat swam after him, shouting, "Stop him! He has not paid the toll or shown his passport!" But the current only rushed on stronger than ever, carrying the little paper boat with it.

The tin soldier could see a light at the end of the tunnel. But he could also hear a terrible roaring sound, loud enough to frighten the bravest man. Below there was a large canal. The water from the drain plunged into it so steeply that it was like a giant waterfall to the little tin soldier. But he could not stop his little boat. Even though he was sure this would be his end, he stood as tall as he could to show that he really was a good soldier. Down tumbled the little boat. It whirled around and around and filled with water. The paper began to break apart, and it was clear that nothing could save the boat from sinking. Soon the little tin soldier was up to his neck in water. As the waves closed over his head, he thought again of the pretty little dancer, and he seemed to hear the words of the old song:

Farewell, true soldier, ever brave,
For now you must come to your grave!

Just then, a great big fish swam by and swallowed him! How dark it was in the fish's belly! Much darker than the tunnel, and much narrower, too. The tin soldier lay still and made sure to hold tightly to his gun. The fish darted this way and that, but then after a while, it became very still. Much later, a great flash of lightning seemed to pass through it, and the tin soldier found himself in bright daylight again. He heard a voice say, "Why, look! Here is the tin soldier!"

The fish had been caught and taken to market. There it had been sold to the cook, who brought it home to the kitchen and cut it open with a big knife. She picked up the tin soldier and carefully carried him upstairs.

Although everyone was eager to see the amazing tin soldier who'd traveled in the belly of a fish, he was not at all proud. They set him down on the table, and—as many strange things happen in this world—he saw that he was back in the very room where he'd started. The same children were standing over him, and the very same toys sat on the table. There was the colored top, the stuffed bear, and, of course, the paper castle.

In the doorway, the pretty little dancer stood on one leg with her other lifted high in the air. She had not moved at all, for she was as steadfast as he. When he saw this, the tin soldier was so touched that if he could he would have wept tears of tin. But instead, he only stared at the little dancer, and she stared back, and neither of them said a word.

All of a sudden, one of the little boys picked up the tin soldier and tossed him into the fire. The goblin must have made him do it, for I can think of no other reason! The flames roared around the little tin soldier. The heat seemed terrible, but whether that was because of the fire or the warmth of his feelings, he could not tell. Soon the bright colors of his uniform faded, but that might have been from sorrow. He looked at the dancer, and she looked back at him. He could 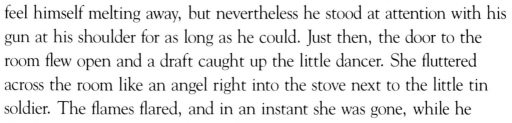 feel himself melting away, but nevertheless he stood at attention with his gun at his shoulder for as long as he could. Just then, the door to the room flew open and a draft caught up the little dancer. She fluttered across the room like an angel right into the stove next to the little tin soldier. The flames flared, and in an instant she was gone, while he slowly melted away into a lump of tin.

The next morning when the maid cleaned the ashes from the stove, she found him in the shape of a little tin heart. All that was left of the dancer was her silver sequin, burned black as coal.

The Emperor's New Clothes

There was once an emperor who loved clothes more than anything else. Unlike other emperors he cared nothing for his soldiers or dancing or the theater. The only thing that made him truly happy was a new suit of clothes. He had a different outfit for every hour of the day. And whenever anyone asked where the emperor was, the reply was almost always, "He is in his dressing room."

Now, one day two swindlers arrived at the city where this emperor lived. Having heard how much the emperor loved clothes, they let it be known that they were weavers and that the cloth they wove was the finest in the world. Not only were the colors and patterns extraordinarily beautiful, but clothes made of this cloth had the remarkable quality of being invisible to anyone who was a fool or unfit for the office he or she held.

Soon the emperor heard about this amazing cloth. "It must be wonderful stuff indeed," he thought. "Why, if I had a suit made of it I should learn which of my ministers were unfit for their positions. I should know who is clever and who is not! I must order a suit of this wonderful cloth at once!" So he summoned the swindlers to his palace that very day, ordered them to begin work at once, and paid them with a big bag of gold.

The two men set up their looms in a large room in the palace. They ordered the finest silk threads. Then they pretended to settle down to work. But actually they only hid the thread and did nothing at all. After a time, they called for more silk and threads of silver and gold. Now they pretended to work even harder and were seen bending over their empty looms late into the night.

"I wonder how the cloth is coming," the emperor thought one day. Then he remembered that the cloth would be invisible to anyone who was unfit for his office, and that made him rather uneasy. Of course, he was sure that he was fit to be emperor, but even so, it might be better to have someone else look at it first. "I'll send my honest old minister to see the weavers," the emperor decided. "He is certainly not a fool, and he knows his office better than anyone in the land."

So the trusted old minister went to the room where the swindlers sat pretending to weave their wonderful cloth. "Good heavens!" the minister thought when he entered and saw the empty looms. He opened his eyes wide and then even wider, but still he could see nothing.

The swindlers begged him to come closer. Pointing at their looms, they asked him about the marvelous colors and the splendid pattern. The minister did not know what to say. "Can it be that I am really a fool?" he thought. "I never would have believed it! Or could I be unfit for my office? That would be dreadful! I must not let the emperor know this!"

"Have you nothing to say?" the swindlers asked him.

"Oh, yes!" replied the minister. "I am just so overwhelmed, you understand! This is the most wonderful cloth I have ever seen! What an exquisite pattern! What brilliant colors! I will tell the emperor at once!"

"We were sure you would like it," the swindlers replied. Then they described the colors and the pattern to him. The old minister listened closely so he would be able to repeat everything to the emperor.

The swindlers then asked for more silk and more thread of gold and silver. As before, they hid all this away so that not a single thread came near their looms, yet they pretended to work day and night.

After a while, the emperor decided to see again how the cloth was coming. "It must be nearly finished by now," he thought. This time he sent his most honest courtier to have a look at it.

Like the minister before him, the courtier opened his eyes wide and then wider. But he, too, could see nothing, for, of course, there was nothing to see.

"I am sure I am no fool," the courtier thought. "Can it be then that I do not deserve the position I hold? What am I to do? I cannot possibly let the emperor know this!" So like the minister before him, he praised the beautiful colors and intricate pattern. "I have never seen anything to compare with it," he told the emperor.

Soon everyone in the city could talk of nothing but the marvelous cloth. At last, the emperor decided he must see it for himself. Surrounded by his courtiers, he went to the room where the two swindlers labored over their empty looms.

"Is it not exquisite?" said the minister and the courtier who had been there before. "What splendid colors! What an amazing pattern!" Then they pointed at the empty looms, certain that all the others could see the wonderful cloth.

The emperor put on his spectacles. Then he stared and stared. "How can this be?" he thought. "I can see nothing! Oh, this is the worst thing that has ever happened to me! Can it be that I am a fool or unfit to be emperor? I must never breathe a word of this!"

"I must thank you," he said out loud, turning to the weavers with a gracious smile. "I have never seen such cloth in all my life!" The emperor's courtiers, who like him could see nothing, all agreed. The cloth, they said, was "exquisite," "magnificent," and "surely the most beautiful in all the world." Then they told the emperor he must order a suit made of it at once to wear at the great procession that was soon to take place. Everyone nodded and clapped enthusiastically. The emperor appointed the two swindlers "Imperial Weavers To The Court" and gave them each a gold medal.

The night before the procession, the two swindlers burned their candles all night. Everyone could see that they were hard at work finishing the emperor's new suit. They cut through the air with their scissors and stitched with needles without any thread. When morning came, they announced, "The emperor's new suit is ready!"

The emperor, followed by his court, went to the swindlers' workroom. When the emperor and his courtiers strode in, the swindlers held up their arms as if holding something and said, "Look! Here is the jacket!" and, "Look! Here are the trousers!" and, "Look! Here is the waistcoat! And here is the elegant train. Each one is as light as a feather so that one does not feel one is wearing anything at all! That's the real beauty of these clothes!"

"Yes, indeed!" all the courtiers agreed.

"Now, if your majesty would please take off your clothes," the swindlers went on, "we will dress you in your new suit!"

They led the emperor to a large looking glass. After he had un-
dressed, the swindlers pretended to put on his new suit piece by piece
while the emperor studied his reflection from all sides.

"How well these new clothes suit you!" everyone cried. "What a perfect fit! That pattern! Those colors! Never have you worn anything so
magnificent!"

It was time for the procession to begin. The servants who were to
carry the train now stepped behind the emperor. They lifted their hands
as though they were holding something. After all, they did not want to
appear to be fools or, worse still, unfit for their positions. Then the emperor began marching at the head of the great procession right through
the city. People lined the streets and leaned out of windows to watch, and
when they saw him pass they all cried, "Isn't the emperor's new suit magnificent? What a gorgeous train! What colors! What a pattern!" No one
dared admit that he could see nothing, for then his neighbors would
know that he was a fool or unfit for his position, and *that* would be dreadful. Never had any clothes of the emperor's been so admired.

At last a child peered through the crowd and cried, "But the emperor
has no clothes!" The mother tried to hush the child, but then she looked
again. "Oh no!" she said. "Can it be true?" Everyone began to whisper
what the child had said. Then they all began to cry out together, "But
the emperor has no clothes!" The emperor heard them, and his ears
turned bright red. He knew that they were right, but there was nothing
he could do. And so the emperor lifted his head higher still and kept on
walking. Even if he had no clothes, he would still carry himself as an
emporer should. And his servants followed behind him, looking even more
dignified than before, carrying in their hands a train that did not exist.

The Princess
and the Pea

O nce upon a time there lived a prince who wished more than anything to find a princess to marry. He traveled far and wide, and although he met many princesses, none of them was quite what he wanted. Some were too stout, some were too tall, some were too serious, and some were too silly. Not one of them was everything a real princess should be. And so the sad prince returned home.

Soon after his return there was a terrible storm. All around the palace, the lightning flashed, the thunder roared, and the rain poured down fiercely. That night there came a knocking at the palace gate, and the old king went to answer it.

A princess stood there, but what a sight she was. Rain streamed from her long hair, and her clothes were muddy and torn. Her shoes were so full of water that it poured out from her toes and heels. Yet she insisted that she was a real princess.

"We'll soon find out if that's true!" thought the old queen, but she said nothing. Instead, she went to a bedchamber and laid a single pea

beneath the mattress. She ordered her servants to pile nineteen more mattresses on top of the pea and twenty eiderdown quilts on top of the mattresses. The queen then led the princess to the bed and bid her good night.

The next morning, the princess was asked how she had slept.

"Oh," she replied, "very badly indeed. I don't know what could have been in that bed, but it was very hard and uncomfortable! I'm black and blue all over! It's terrible!"

And then everyone in the palace knew that she must be a real princess, for she had felt the pea right through twenty mattresses and twenty eiderdown quilts. Surely, only a real princess could do that!

So the prince took her for his wife because he knew that she was a real princess, and they lived very happily together. As for the pea, it was put in the museum, where it can still be seen.

And so ends a true story.

The Little Match Girl

I t was the last evening of the year, and it was very cold and dark. Snowflakes fell thick and fast. Through the empty streets wandered a poor little girl with no hat on her head and no shoes on her feet. When she left home that morning she had been wearing a pair of slippers. But they were so large that she'd lost them as she'd dashed across the street to avoid a huge carriage rolling toward her. One of the slippers had disappeared, and a young boy had picked up the other and run off with it. So the little girl was barefoot, and her feet were now blue with cold. In her hands she carried a bundle of matches, and the pockets of her apron were stuffed with them. All day long she tried to sell her matches, but no one had bought a single one or given her a single penny. Shivering with cold and hunger, she crept along the icy streets. Lights shone in all the windows, and the air was full of the delicious aroma of roast goose, a reminder that it was New Year's Eve. At last, in a corner between two houses, she sank down, pulled her feet under her, and huddled close to the wall. Still she could not keep off the cold.

She dared not go home, for she hadn't sold a single match, and she was certain her father would beat her. Besides, home was not much warmer than the cold street, for the walls were full of holes. Her father had stuffed the largest of them with straw and rags, but the wind still howled through day and night.

So the little girl remained near the wall, her hands almost frozen with cold. "How much good a single match would do!" she thought. Would she dare to pull one from the bundle and strike it against the wall? She did—Sprrrt! It burst into flame, and as it burned it gave off a warm clear light like a candle. The little match girl held out her hand to the beautiful brightness. It seemed as if she were sitting by a big iron stove with polished brass feet and a glowing brass door. The fire blazed and sputtered. It looked so real that the child stretched out her feet to warm them. Just then the match flickered, the brass stove vanished, and the little girl was left holding only the half-burnt match in her hand.

Quickly she struck another. It flared, shining on the wall, which in an instant became transparent as glass. Through it the little girl could see a warm, brightly lit room. There was a table covered with a snow-white cloth. On it were fine china plates and glass goblets, and in the center was a steaming roast goose stuffed with apples and prunes. Then an amazing thing happened. The goose leaped from its dish and, with a knife and fork still in its breast, came waddling toward the little match girl. Before the girl could taste the goose, the match went out, and she found herself again staring at the cold stone wall.

She lit another match. This time she was sitting under a beautiful Christmas tree. It was taller and more brightly decorated than any she had glimpsed through the windows of the rich merchants' houses. Thousands of candles glowed among its green branches, and colored pictures, like those she'd seen in the shop windows, shimmered around it. The little match girl stretched out her hands toward the tree, and then the match went out.

The lights of the Christmas tree seemed to rise higher and higher until the little girl realized she was looking at the twinkling stars in the sky. Then she saw one fall, leaving a bright trail of light behind it. "Someone must be dying," thought the little girl, for her dead grandmother, who was the only person who had ever truly loved her, had once told her that whenever a star falls a soul goes to heaven.

She struck another match against the wall. This time in the center of the bright light stood her grandmother. Her face looked so gentle and loving that the little girl cried out, "Oh Grandmother, please take me with you. I know that when the match blows out you will go away just like the warm stove and the roast goose and the lovely Christmas tree. Please take me with you!"

The little match girl quickly lit the whole bundle of matches, for she so wanted her grandmother to stay with her. And the matches flared with a light that was brighter than the noon sun. Never had her grandmother looked so beautiful. She took the little girl in her arms, and together, they rose far above the cold streets and the dark town to where there was no hunger and no pain, for they climbed all the way to heaven.

The next morning, some people found the little match girl still sitting against the stone wall. Her cheeks were pale, and her little hands were blue, and she was smiling. She'd frozen to death on the last night of the year, and in her hand was the bundle of burnt matches. "The poor child," people said. "She must have tried to warm herself." But none of them could know what beautiful things she had seen, nor with what joy she had entered into the New Year with her grandmother.

Thumbelina

T here was once a woman who for many years longed to have a child, but none came. At last, she went to visit a good fairy and begged her to help. "Here is a barleycorn," the fairy said. "Plant it in a flowerpot and water it well. Then see what happens."

The woman did as she was told. Soon a large and very beautiful flower came up. It looked something like a tulip, but its petals were closed as though it were still a bud. "How lovely it is," the woman said, kissing it. As she did so the red and gold petals opened. Inside was a pretty little maiden only half as tall as the woman's thumb. The woman and her husband were overjoyed and named the child Thumbelina.

The child's cradle was a polished walnut shell with a violet petal for a pillow and a rose petal for a coverlet. Here she slept each night. During the day she played on the table where the woman had placed a plateful of water. Using a tulip petal as a boat and two white horsehairs as oars, Thumbelina rowed herself around and around the tiny lake. As she rowed, she sang to herself in the loveliest little voice imaginable.

One night as Thumbelina lay in her tiny bed, a great ugly toad crept through the open window. "What a pretty little maiden," the toad croaked when she saw Thumbelina. "She'd make a fine wife for my son!" Picking up the little walnut cradle, she carried Thumbelina away to her home in the marsh.

The toad's son was even bigger and uglier than his mother. When he saw the little maiden he croaked with delight.

"Shhh! You'll wake her," his mother scolded. "We'd better put her on a lily pad in the middle of the stream. That way she won't be able to run away." So the old toad swam out to the largest lily pad, and on it she placed the little walnut cradle with Thumbelina inside.

The next morning when Thumbelina awoke, she found herself on the great lily pad and water all around. She began to cry. She could not see any way of getting back to dry land. Soon the two big ugly toads came swimming up to the lily pad.

"Here is my son," the mother toad croaked. "He is to be your husband. I am preparing a lovely home for you down in the mud."

"Croak! Croak!" was all the son could say.

After they left, Thumbelina began to weep bitterly. She didn't want to marry the ugly toad and live with him in the muddy marsh. Some little fish swimming in the stream heard her sobbing. They lifted their heads out of the water to look at her. When they saw how sad Thumbelina was, they felt sorry for her. "A pretty maiden like that marry an ugly toad!" they cried. "It cannot be!" So they gathered under the lily pad and began gnawing at the stalk. At last, the stem broke and Thumbelina floated away downstream.

She sailed past forests, green pastures, and big bustling towns. The birds in the bushes looked down at her and sang, "How pretty the maiden is!"

A beetle, who was flying overhead, spotted Thumbelina as she floated down the stream. He swooped down and seized her in his claws and carried her to his nest high in a tree. He put Thumbelina down on a leaf at the top of the tree, and he settled beside her. He told her she was very pretty, though she didn't look at all like a beetle, and he said he would like to make her his wife. Presently, the other beetles came over to meet Thumbelina. But when they saw her, they turned up their feelers in horror. "How strange and ugly she is!" they cried. "Why, she has only two legs and no feelers at all! Why, she looks just like a human being!"

When he heard what the others said, the beetle who had brought Thumbelina there wanted nothing more to do with her. He flew her down from the tree and set her on a daisy. Here, Thumbelina began to cry because she thought she was too ugly for even a beetle to want, though, of course, she was prettier than the prettiest rose!

The whole summer Thumbelina lived all alone in the forest. She wove herself a bed of grass, then hung it under a big leaf to keep off the rain. She ate the nectar from the flowers and drank the dew from the leaves. Autumn came and went, and before long it was winter.

The birds who had sung to her all summer flew away. The leaves fell from the trees, and all the flowers wilted and died. Thumbelina no longer had a protected place to hang her bed. Then it began to snow. Poor Thumbelina almost froze to death. She was so small, and compared to her, the snowflakes were so big that they nearly buried her. She wrapped herself in a dry leaf to keep warm, but still she shivered.

At last, she set off through the woods. Soon she came to a large cornfield and the home of a field mouse under the corn roots. The field mouse lived in warmth and comfort. A fire heated the kitchen, and the storerooms were stocked with corn. Shivering, Thumbelina knocked on the door and begged for something to eat.

"Oh, you poor thing," cried the field mouse when she saw the pretty little maiden. "Come in and have some supper with me." After they had eaten, the field mouse said, "If you will cook and clean for me, and tell me nice stories, you may stay with me for as long as you like."

Thumbelina happily agreed, and soon she was living in great comfort.

"We are going to have a visitor," the field mouse said one day. "He is much wealthier than I am, and he wears a beautiful black waistcoat. Oh, he would make you a fine husband, Thumbelina! But he is blind, so you must be sure and tell him one of your most amusing stories."

The visitor came. He certainly was rich, and there could be no doubt that he knew many things. But Thumbelina was not very interested in him because he was a mole. Moreover, he made fun of the flowers and the sun, which he had never seen. Still, to please the field mouse, she told him her best stories and sang for him in her sweet, clear voice. The mole soon fell in love with her, though he didn't say anything, for he was a very cautious gentleman.

Now the mole had recently dug a long tunnel between his house and the field mouse's. One day he invited the field mouse and Thumbelina to pay him a visit and offered to guide them through the tunnel himself. "But you must not be alarmed by the dead bird that lies in the passage," he told them.

So they set out. When they came to where the dead bird lay, the mole pushed his nose up through the ceiling of the tunnel by accident. The earth caved in, letting the sun shine through.

In the light, Thumbelina could clearly see the dead bird. It was a swallow. He didn't look as if he'd been dead long. His wings were pulled close to his sides, and his head was tucked under his feathers. "Poor bird!" Thumbelina thought. "He must have died of the cold." She thought of all the birds who had sung to her so beautifully all summer and felt very sad.

The mole pushed the swallow aside. "He certainly won't sing again," he said. "Thank goodness my children won't be birds! What's the good of singing all summer if you only die of cold when winter comes?"

"That is very true," agreed the field mouse politely.

Thumbelina said nothing, but when the other two turned their backs, she quickly bent over and kissed the swallow. "Farewell, dear pretty bird," she whispered. "Perhaps it was you who sang so prettily to me all summer long."

That night, however, Thumbelina could not sleep. At last, she got out of bed and wove a thick blanket of hay. This she carried to the dead swallow and carefully covered him with it. "Farewell, pretty bird," she whispered, laying her head on the bird's chest. She was startled! She heard a loud thumping noise! It was the bird's heart. He was not really dead but only in a faint from the cold. Thumbelina couldn't help feeling frightened because the swallow was much larger than she. But she bravely wrapped the blanket tightly around him and tiptoed away.

The next night Thumbelina again visited the swallow. He was alive but very weak. "Thank you for saving me," he whispered. "Perhaps I can fly out into the sunshine."

"Oh, no," Thumbelina replied. "It's still very cold. Keep still and I will take care of you until spring comes." So for the rest of the winter, she tenderly nursed the swallow.

At last, spring came and the swallow was well enough to fly. Thumbelina opened the hole the mole had made, and the warm sunlight came

shining through. It looked so beautiful that the swallow begged Thumbelina to come away with him. She could sit on his back, he said. He would fly with her into the green woods. But Thumbelina said no. She did not want to hurt the field mouse's feelings by leaving her that way.

"Good-bye then, my little friend," the swallow said, spreading his wings and soaring into the blue sky.

Thumbelina watched him go. Tears came into her eyes. How she longed to follow him into the bright sunlight! But she could not.

The corn sprouted, and all summer it grew high and strong until it was like a thick wood to Thumbelina. "Come!" the field mouse told her. "We must prepare your wedding dress, Thumbelina. The mole has asked for your hand in marriage!"

Now Thumbelina had to sit spinning day and night. The field mouse hired four spiders to help her so that the dress would be finished in time. Every evening the mole came to call. He made Thumbelina sing "Bye-bye, Ladybird" and other songs for him. He told her they would get married as soon as summer was over.

Thumbelina was most upset, for she did not wish to marry the mole at all. Every morning when the sun rose, and every evening as it set, she tiptoed to the field mouse's door and gazed out at the warm sun and the bright blue sky. Then she would sigh. She longed to see her friend the swallow just one more time.

At last, as the autumn wind blew across the corn, Thumbelina's wedding dress was finished. "You will be married the day after tomorrow!" the field mouse happily told her.

Thumbelina burst into tears. "I don't want to marry the mole!" she cried.

"Don't be silly, or I'll bite you with my sharp teeth," the field mouse said curtly. "He is very handsome and rich as well. You should be grateful to have such a suitor!"

Thumbelina felt very sad. She knew that after she married the mole, she would never again see the sun and the flowers or hear the birds sing. Drying her tears, she went outside one last time.

"Farewell, beautiful sun!" she whispered. "Farewell!" She hugged a small red flower growing just beside the door. "Say hello to the swallow for me if you ever see him again!"

"Tweet, tweet," cried the swallow, who was just overhead and had come especially to see her. Thumbelina was overjoyed to see her friend, and she told him how she was to marry the mole and live underground where the sun never shone.

"Come with me instead," the swallow replied. "I am flying south for the winter. You may sit on my back and tie yourself to my feathers with your sash. We will leave behind forever the gloomy mole and his dark passages. I will take you to warm places where the sun shines even more brightly than it does here and the flowers are always in bloom. Please come! I have never forgotten how you saved my life when I lay frozen in that dark tunnel!"

"Yes! I will come!" Thumbelina said. She climbed on the swallow's back, tied her scarf around one of his feathers, and together they soared high in the air.

The swallow flew with her over great forests, shining seas, and high mountains blanketed by snow. They passed through warm, pleasant lands where purple and green grapes grew and the air smelled of oranges and lemons.

At last, they came to a clear blue lake. Beside it, surrounded by tall green trees, stood a palace of gleaming white marble. On the roof were many swallows' nests, and Thumbelina could hear all the birds singing.

"This is my home," said the swallow. "But you would not be happy in a rooftop nest. Instead, I will place you in one of those flowers below."

On the ground lay a large white marble column broken in three pieces, and among the pieces there grew the most lovely white flowers. The swallow placed Thumbelina on the largest of them, and what a surprise she had when she looked around. She could hardly believe her eyes! A tiny little man, as transparent as if he were made of crystal, stood in the middle of the flower. On his head he wore a tiny gold crown, and two delicate little wings grew from his shoulders. He was the fairy of the flower—for in every flower lives either a tiny man or woman fairy, and this little man was king of all the flower fairies.

When he saw Thumbelina he thought she was by far the most beautiful creature he had ever seen. He asked her name, and then he asked if she would be his wife. He was nothing like the ugly toad, the beetle, or the mole, and so Thumbelina delightedly said, "Yes."

All the flowers happily opened, and each flower fairy brought Thumbelina a gift, the best of which was a pair of tiny gossamer wings. These the flower fairies fastened to Thumbelina's shoulders so she, too, could flit from flower to flower just as they did.

That spring the wedding of Thumbelina and the fairy king was celebrated with great joy. The swallow sang a wedding song, the most beautiful song you can imagine. It was both a happy and sad song, for the swallow was bidding farewell to his dear friend Thumbelina. It was time to return to his northern home. "Farewell, farewell," he cried as he took flight.

Now, every spring the swallow sings of Thumbelina, and that is how we came to hear her story.